BANQUETS & BOOTLEG BOUNTY

Lily Barrish Levner

Neversink Press

Catskills Capers Book 1
Banquets & Bootleg Bounty
Copyright 2024 By Lily Barrish Levner

ISBN 979-8-9908952-0-1

Printed in the United States of America

Published by
Neversink Press
South Fallsburg, New York

Cover design by Sweet 'N Spicy Designs

Yiddish Dictionary

Alta cocker: older person
Bashert: meant to be
Boychik: boy
Bubbe: grandmother
Bruchas: blessing/prayer
Chazer: a pig, greedy person
Farpitst: dressed up to the nines
Fartick: the end/done/full
Fleishigs: meat-based meal
Gelt: money
Genug iz genug: enough is enough
Gonif: thief
Gonsa macher: big, important person
Goy: Non-Jewish person
Kaddish: Jewish prayer said in honor of the dead
Kinder: children
Kvetch: whining/complaining
Ligner: liar
Mazel tov: congratulations or good luck
Mensch: person of integrity
Meshuga: crazy
Milkhik: dairy-based meal
Oy vey: (oh, woe!) dismay, frustration, grief
Paskudnyak: contemptible person
Pesach: Passover
Putz: foolish/jerk
Schlep: drag or carry
Schmaltz: rendered chicken fat
Schmata: rag

Schmear: to spread
Schmooze: chat
Schmuck: obnoxious person
Schtick: act/gimmick/trick/prank
Shabbat Shalom: a sabbath greeting
Shadchante: a woman matchmaker
Shayna: beautiful
Shekel: Hebrew word for coin
Shiva: seven days of mourning
Shtarker: gangster/hard man
Shtetl: little town
Shtick drek: piece of shit
Shvitzing: sweating
Taam: taste
Treif: unkosher
Tuchus: buttocks
Tummler: comic entertainer
Verklempt: choked up
Yagde: blueberries
Zayde: grandfather
Zhlub: big clumsy person

A Short History of the Glory Days of the Hotel Industry & Murder, Inc.

The years 1940-1965 were the height of the hotel industry in the Catskill Mountains. An estimated 500+ hotels and resorts existed throughout the area during that time. Bungalow colonies, boarding houses, and summer camps dotted the mountain landscape.

The guests were predominantly Jewish, banned at many other resorts but welcomed in the Catskills. The staff comprised immigrants, refugees, and people seeking the American Dream. It was the Golden Era.

But amidst the games and gaiety, the Big Bands and banquets, there was also a darker side. Murder, Inc., the enforcement arm of the national crime syndicates of the era, was active from 1929 until 1941. Most of the members were Italian and Jewish boys from New York City. They were known as notorious killers for hire, triggermen without a conscience, and cold-hearted enforcers. Louis Buchalter led the organized crime group until his execution in 1944.

The mountains were popular stomping grounds for Murder, Inc. Sometimes innocent people unknowingly got involved and this is where our story begins.

SUMMER 1944

The hotel lit the mountain terrain as the automobile left the premises. After hurtling around several blind curves on country roads, the car finally stopped near a farmhouse. A man sprinted into the moonless night and crept around the farm. He stopped by a shed; the chilly spring air made him shiver. Listening to the eerie lowing of a cow, he began to dig...

CHAPTER 1
Week 1, Friday

DOTTY

"That sure is a fancy ride," a passerby called and whistled while a black Buick Roadmaster rolled to a stop next to the curb on E. 167th Street.

Dotty fanned herself with one hand and clutched the handle of her large, olive-green bag with the other. She was winded and *shvitzing* after she *schlepped* from her family's third-floor walk-up apartment during a Bronx heat wave.

Cars zipped past, and the elevated Jerome Avenue subway rumbled along the tracks. She said, "Good riddance" to the concrete and brick buildings she was leaving behind. It was thrilling to escape the city heat for a couple of months.

Just last night, she had been surprised when Papa told her there was a seat available in the taxicab. She planned to take the bus. She waved goodbye to the neighborhood, flashing a sunny smile over her good fortune. A hack was such a decadent way to travel to the mountains.

"The middle seat is open," said the driver, rearranging luggage in the trunk.

A gentleman stood outside the car so she could crawl into the center of the three-person bench seat. She rested her handbag on her lap and settled in for an adventure. "I can't believe I'm going to the Concord!"

"Oh, the Concord," the silver-haired woman sitting to her left said in a dreamy voice. "I'm going to the Heiden Hotel in South Fallsburg."

"I'm visiting my aunt and uncle at the Hotel Evans in Loch Sheldrake for the weekend," volunteered the gentleman, who was back inside the car, sitting to her right.

"We've got one more stop to fetch a wife staying at Sunny Oaks bungalow colony in South Fallsburg for the next two months. Her husband won't be in the mountains until next week," the driver said, speeding off.

"Are we in a vaudeville act?" Dotty asked a few minutes later. She watched the middle-aged woman bringing out suitcases, food, a lamp, an ironing board, dishes, pans, and sheets. It seemed she had packed her entire city apartment.

The driver huffed and puffed as he tied a rope around the roof rack. The lamp wobbled, a casserole dish crashed, and a flock of pigeons hijacked a loaf of bread.

Once everything was loaded and everyone was seated, the driver was chatty. "It's the first year the Concord has been open year-round."

"I've heard wonderful things about it." Dotty shimmied her shoulders, gazing at the scenery roll by. "I'm one of the first waitresses under the new maître d', Irving Cohen."

The driver removed one hand from the wheel to snap his fingers. "You are going to a happening place. How'd you end up at Arthur Winarick's masterpiece?"

"My papa said you can make real nice money in the mountains. So, I went to an employment agency down in the Bowery. Since most boys are off at war, they are desperate to hire workers."

"I've stayed at Grossinger's. Never at the Concord," said the gentleman heading to Hotel Evans.

"The Grossingers are the reason I have such a thriving business. They attracted the vacationers to the Catskills. People love to stay under Jennie Grossinger's roof. They don't call it the 'Waldorf of the Catskills' for nothing," said the driver.

Dozens of people had mentioned Grossinger's to her after learning she would be waitressing in the mountains. She pictured a stately hotel sitting on sprawling grounds.

The driver snapped his fingers again. "Here's a little mountain history for you. Grossinger's was the most lavish resort until your new boss, Arthur Winarick, cropped up with a fortune in hand. One night he couldn't get a room at the G because the hotel was booked. Right then and there he vowed to build a bigger and better hotel to lure the guests away. After the prior owner of the Ideal House defaulted, he lucked out and acquired it. Renamed it and rebuilt it. That's how the Concord started. There were thirty guests in the beginning and look at it already—there are three hundred guests now."

"It's true. Grossinger's has the name recognition, but the Concord has the finances," said the woman heading to Sunny Oaks.

"Every building at the Concord was designed to meet Winarick's vision of richness," said the Heiden Hotel guest.

"Bet you didn't know that Winarick bought concrete and steel structures in their entirety from the

1939 World's Fair. He also purchased a ferryboat at 125th Street and dismantled it for steel. He didn't have to borrow a penny," the driver said, veering to the left.

"How did he become so wealthy?" Dotty asked.

"Winarick was a barber during Prohibition. He's one lucky son of a gun. On account of his profession, he had rights to alcohol, and his brother just so happened to be a chemist. They set up a basement barber shop. Sold bootleg liquor on the side and made a killing selling Jeris Hair Tonic—largely consisting of alcohol and perfume."

"He's a real clever man," she said.

The driver sang the jingle, "Jeris hits the jackpot for greaseless good grooming and healthier, handsomer hair."

She had high hopes that her pockets would soon be overflowing with tips and she would be able to buy Papa some of the hair tonic for his birthday.

"It's hot in here!" shouted the wife in the front, fanning herself with a handkerchief.

"Roll down a window!" shouted the gentleman in the back.

"The wind is blowing on me," complained the wife.

Dotty raised her hand and caught the silver-haired woman's pillbox hat before it flew out the window. The woman sighed in relief.

"Have you considered trying out for the Yankees with a catch like that?" asked the driver.

She smiled and leaned her head back. She remembered the one time her family had stayed at the Delano Hotel in Monticello. She loved playing the pinball machine there.

About midway through their trip, coasting on the narrow, two-lane Route 17 highway, the hack turned off and into the crowded parking lot of the Red Apple Rest. Dotty stared at the large red apple that sat on top of the roof as they waited for an overheated car's engine to spring back to life. Once the parking space opened, she sprinted under the multicolored striped awning. Astonished by the impressive roadside eatery, she surveyed the wide selection of hot and cold food. Papa had told her the washrooms here were the nicest public ones anywhere. He had also said Reuben Freed, the owner, showed genuine care for his patrons. The outdoor line for frankfurters and ice cream was long, so she settled on a root beer soda pop from inside. She did not have an appetite anyway. The lively waystation made her even more excited to reach her destination.

They drove through Chester and Goshen. In Middletown, the traffic became bottlenecked on the winding streets. From Middletown, they traveled back roads. At the bottom of the Wurtsboro mountain, the hack was so overloaded she feared they would not clear the hill.

ABE

Riveted by all the billboards lining the country roads directing guests to the Catskill Mountain resorts, Abe kept his nose pressed to the window. As the black Buick Super wound through towns and villages that made up Sullivan County, he saw bungalow renters unloading their jam-packed vehicles and airing out their summer bungalows. They were his first glimpse of summer vacationers in the mountains.

A rectangular-shaped building painted a buttery shade of yellow with brown trim came into view. The Buick skidded to a halt in front of it, and the driver said, "You can make a real comfortable living here. Arthur Winarick created something special."

Abe jerked forward and his glasses slid down his face. It was a grand version of the architecture he was used to back in Brighton Beach. He counted the windows on the four-story building that could stretch the length of three Brooklyn blocks as he crawled out of the back seat. He ran his eyes over the lush landscape, inhaling fresh mountain air, already filled with respect for this Arthur Winarick fella. Exquisite gardens and dense trees lined the pristine grounds. Crystal-clear Kiamesha Lake, to the left of the main building, faced the perfectly maintained nine holes of the golf course.

Three entertainers were wedged together in the backseat, surrounded by costumes and props that would not fit into the overstuffed trunk. He retrieved his bag from under wigs, cards, and a top hat. "My pockets might not be full yet, but I'm only returning home once they are overflowing," he vowed, waving goodbye to the fella behind the wheel who'd given him a lift to the mountains. He spent the entire ride memorizing every piece of advice he received, determined to make a success of himself with the fortuitous opportunities in front of him.

He threw his shoulders back and held his head high. He fit right in. Back in New York City, the lack of men on the streets made him ashamed that people believed he was a malingerer not returning to war. The doors to the hotel were pulling him to something special. He followed the bustling bellhops and energized guests into the lobby.

Luggage began to pile up in front of the doorway while he waited for his room assignment in the staff living quarters. An unassuming man wearing a white shirt, suspenders, and faded pants hurried over to haul the suitcases to a corner, so Abe trooped over to help. He stacked suitcases one on top of another, presuming the man must be an older lobby porter and well-liked since everyone who passed by smiled his way.

After they stacked all the suitcases, the man stuck his hand out. "Thank you. I can already tell you're a hard worker. I'm Arthur Winarick. Welcome to my hotel."

His heartbeat doubled its normal rhythm. He expected a sharp-dressed *gonsa macher*, not just an ordinary fella with thinning hair and lackluster clothing.

Already counting his luck, he received his room assignment and trekked the short distance to the staff living quarters, a separate hotel called the Colonial. It sat behind the main hotel where the guests stayed. The white-painted building reminded him of an oversized bungalow. He let out a low whistle as he pushed into the first-floor room.

A boy with wavy brown hair and a polite smile said, "I'm Leon."

Introducing himself, he took the bed on the left since Leon had already chosen the one on the right.

"Hello, Abe. Where did you travel from?"

"Brighton Beach. And you?" He inspected the empty drawers of the dresser. He omitted that he had grown up in Philadelphia, only moving to Brooklyn once his mother had reappeared.

"I'm from Warsaw. I escaped at the start of the war."

Speechless, he unzipped his bag. He knew Poland was thousands of miles away and Leon's journey must have been dangerous. His childhood in foster care had been no picnic, but Leon's life in Europe had presented greater challenges. He tossed a pair of socks into the drawer.

Leon continued. "I was working at a luncheonette in Manhattan, struggling to make a living, when I heard they needed help in the hotels. Can you believe I was completely unaware that there were hills north of the city?"

He had previously traveled to upstate New York, so he was familiar with the countryside. He pulled more socks from his bag. "As soon as I heard about the high wages and all the luxuries that came with living in the mountains, I signed up on the spot. I prefer this to being cooped up inside my stepfather's garment factory all day. I didn't expect such a dandy space to call home for the summer."

"How come you aren't enrolled in the army?"

He shifted his eyes to the single window in the middle of the room. "They discharged me."

Leon remained quiet. His kind eyes encouraged Abe to say more.

"I was a drill sergeant in Miami until a doctor diagnosed my eyesight as too poor to continue to serve." He returned from duty, at 19 years old, with his brunette hair a shade more golden, his skin tanned, and his muscles bulging from a year of physical activity under the Florida sun.

"There is no shame in wearing spectacles."

He tapped the rim of his glasses. "My eyesight isn't that terrible."

Leon reached for his checkered newsboy hat; his voice was friendly. "Ah, a Jewish doctor who didn't want to see another Jewish boy come home in a coffin."

He raked his hands through his hair, swallowing hard. Here he was a young man in perfect health, while both of his brothers were still serving in the U.S Army. He never wanted people to think he was less patriotic. His Ma's words rang in his ears. "Abe-*ala*, this means I won't lose all three of my boys."

That comment had stung.

"The Concord is lucky to have you."

He snapped back to the present. "I have had the pleasure of meeting the owner already."

Leon's eyebrows shot toward the ceiling. "Arthur Winarick? Making a good impression right away is smart." He pointed to his head. "I made sure to use Jeris Hair Tonic today in case I bumped into him. That's why my hair is so glossy."

He scratched his ear, not admitting he did not understand the reference. "How come you speak such fluent English?"

"I had a neighbor back in Poland who was a diplomat and a resistance fighter. He taught English classes." Leon placed the newsboy cap on top of his head.

Sprawled out on his mattress, stretching his legs and wiggling his toes, Abe knew he had made the right decision. And he was glad he had someone like Leon by his side. "I feel like a king."

"There's tremendous potential."

His smile spread from ear to ear. "I think I can pave my own way up here."

A whole new chapter was beginning.

DOTTY

Dotty tried to read every single one of the hotel billboards cramming the landscape. When they approached the sign that said, "Turn Here to Concord Hotel," she was jiggling her legs.

The Hotel Evans guest hollered, "Can you drop me off first?"

"I have specific directions. She's number one on the list." The driver tilted his head toward the woman en route to the Heiden.

At the first drop-off, Dotty could not take her eyes off the Tudor-style building as the driver announced, "The Concord is the next stop."

Now she could not sit still.

Minutes later, after zooming up the mountain, the driver said, "We've arrived. Good luck." He handed her olive-green bag over.

"The Bronx has no space that compares to this." She gawked in awe at the size of the building nestled in rich grounds.

The yellow paint on the exterior reminded her of their kitchen's wallpaper at home. Oh, she could not wait to tell Ma and Papa about this exquisite place. Her parents, Merke and Isaac, expected her to write to them all summer long. She would send a postcard soon.

She took a moment to smell the sweet floral scent from the colorful flower gardens before she *schlepped* her bag through the entryway. People crowded the lobby, greeting each other as long-lost friends. Some staff were new hires, like herself. Others were returning for another season in the mountains.

A helpful bellhop tapped her on the shoulder. "I'll carry your bag to the Colonial, where you'll be staying." He led her to another building.

She blinked hard. "I get to live here? It's an entire hotel!"

"Staff living conditions like this certainly aren't the norm. Nobody sleeps on a cot in a closet around here. Arthur makes sure we have the best."

"I'm so lucky the Concord hired me." She watched two fellas stride into the Colonial.

"It's coed," said the bellhop, winking.

She raised her eyebrows, never having stayed in co-ed living quarters. She stepped into her new home. The blue and white floral wallpaper caught her eye. Her papa, who worked as a wallpaper hanger, always made sure to do careful work. He would be pleased with the job done here.

Once she reached her assigned room, she straightened her skirt and blouse. A striking girl with chestnut-colored curls appeared in the doorway. "I heard you thumping down the hallway. Welcome. I'm Eva. I'm a waitress in the main dining room. Do you play cards? How about poker?"

She plopped her bag onto the ground and sat on the empty bed to catch her breath. "I'm a waitress as well. Yes, I love playing cards." She ran her hands through her dishwater-blonde hair, wishing it had as much volume as Eva's.

"I'm organizing a Sunday night game, after we collect our tips, of course." Eva touched the opal heart-shaped stone hanging on a gold chain she wore around her neck.

"I'll be at the table," Dotty promised. She would have to ask Ma for some hints since Ma played cards every day on the Grand Concourse back home in the Bronx.

"Very good. We'll be working hard, but don't worry, there's lots of time for socializing."

She began unpacking as Eva peppered her with questions. "Do you have experience waiting tables?"

"Oh, yes. I learned everything I know at the Lido Beach Hotel on Long Island. I spent a season there before the Navy turned it into an amphibious base and discharge center. I worked at a resort in Far Rockaway and another one out in Lakewood, New Jersey, after that."

Eva put her hands on her hips. "How old were you when you started waitressing?"

"14," she admitted. "I told the man I was 17 and he told me to say 18." She chuckled at the memory. She had worn high heels and bright red lipstick, clomping down Skid Row to the employment agency in the Bowery. Today she was 18 years old and did not have to fib about her age to work at the Concord.

"You're an old pro," Eva said, sweeping her hand through the air.

"How long have you been waitressing?" Dotty, too, had questions.

"After I traveled over from Germany, Arthur Winarick hired me. That was *Pesach* (Passover) two seasons ago."

"Are you a refugee?" She placed her hand over her heart.

"Yes. I'm very lucky to be here. My German mom and British dad raised me in Southern Germany. I'm an English citizen. My parents wanted me out of Europe. They felt it was safest for me to come over to the States. Arthur has a soft spot in his heart for refugees. I landed at the right hotel."

Glad about that, Dotty rested her head on the pillow, enjoying the comfort of her own bed for the first time. She stretched out her legs and closed her eyes. "I've shared the sleeper sofa with my sister and listened to the Jerome Avenue train my entire life."

"You've spent the day traveling; a snooze before Shabbat dinner might set you right."

She jumped back up and parted the curtains to gaze at the greenery. "I hope Irving Cohen isn't too strict."

Eva flung her wrist in the air. "People call him 'King Cupid.' How harsh do you think a man with that nickname can be?"

"What if, since it's his first summer in charge of the dining room, he's extra tough?" She took a deep breath.

"Bet you didn't know he was recently married. Consider him still in the honeymoon phase. Act confident and you'll do fine."

"I've always received compliments from my bosses. I'm not worried." She bit her bottom lip and watched Eva study her reflection in a handheld mirror.

Eva had a twinkle in her eye. "Stay away from Hershel. He's my *bashert*."

Suddenly, Dotty cared a lot more about her appearance as she slipped into her white waitressing uniform. For breakfast and lunch, the two dairy meals of the day, the required dress code was yellow dresses and white aprons. The meat dinner was served wearing white dresses and white aprons.

Eva wiggled into her uniform. "Don't forget the trick is to stay ahead of everything and not lose control of your station. What are the three important terms to measure success?"

"'A breeze' means the meal ran smoothly, a 'good meal' needs no explanation, and a 'bomb' means everything went terribly." She spritzed Chantilly perfume onto her right wrist. The fruity notes of orange blossom mixed with jasmine and other citruses filled their room.

"Very good. What's the worst thing you can do?"

"Anger the chef. I must wait until several guests ask for things from the kitchen. I want to avoid making too many trips back there."

"What's the second-worst thing?"

"I can't get hung up, or I'll never meet all the guests' demands, and I'll fall behind the kitchen's schedule."

"I don't have to tell you tips depend on how pleasant we are to guests and how quickly we feed them."

Thankful for all she learned that first summer on Lido Beach, and confident in her food-serving abilities, Dotty swung the door open. The same two fellas she had seen earlier were now exiting their room a couple of doors down. They wore stark white jackets. *I have a feeling this is going to be a very good summer.*

Chapter 2

ABE

Abe was dressed in the required white bussing jacket with green on the lapel over a white shirt with a black bow tie, black pants, and black shoes. He scanned the sumptuous main dining room that seated hundreds of guests. Wall-length curtains of classic gold lamé complemented the golden upholstered chairs.

His glasses fogged up as soon as he entered the commercial kitchen. The humidity matched one of the worst August days in Brighton Beach. A mixture of smells had his nose sniffing in all directions. Gigantic silver soup kettles where fluffy, golf ball-sized matzo balls floated in savory broth were being heated on the stove. Mouth-watering, ceremonial challah loaves made of eggs and flour lined the counter.

Amazed by the abundance of nosh offered so freely, he recalled the days of his childhood. The food barely stretched to feed all the family members at the table.

Irving Cohen, the commanding, round-faced maître d', wore a black suit and tie. He cleared his throat and spoke to his staff. "The hotel has sold out. Guests arrive at the Concord expecting the staff to serve them luxury every night. Activities, though first-rate, come second. Eating is always first. Do your best to keep every one of them happy."

After his speech, Irving made his rounds, stopping in front of Abe. Pointing to a slender, chestnut-haired waitress, he said, "I'm assigning you to Eva's station tonight. She's a competent waitress. Don't hesitate to ask her for help if you need it." Irving assigned Leon to the waitress standing beside Eva.

"Welcome to the life of a mountain rat," Eva said. "Do you know how special it is to be a busboy under Irving Cohen? He gets the pick of the litter. You have to be whip-smart or he'll fire you after the first meal. There's no harder worker. He's a Russian Jewish immigrant from the Lower East Side."

"I guess I am officially a mountain rat." Abe grinned over the term given to people who lived and worked in Sullivan County. He appreciated the education he was getting and soaked in as much information as he could.

As they set the silverware onto a white-clothed table, Eva said, "I'm terrified the whole table will order the chow mein. A tray full of chow mein would be too heavy for me to carry along with everything else."

"I'll carry the tray for you if that's the case."

She rewarded him with a toothy grin. "I see you already understand the code up here—help your coworkers and in return, they'll help you. Here's the real trick to survival in the mountains: move fast, don't miss a beat, and get things done."

Now that he knew his main responsibility was to assist the waitress at his assigned station, and tips depended on how well he did that, he held his chin up. He was confident he would master the job in no time.

"On Sunday night, we're playing poker. I hope you'll join us." Eva tugged at the heart-shaped necklace she was wearing.

"I enjoy a good card game." He removed his glasses and wiped them clean on his shirttail. *Did Eva have a fella?*

DOTTY

A busboy introduced himself. "I'm Leon, and I'll be assisting you tonight."

Dotty recognized him as one of the fellas she had seen around and greeted him with a warm smile. Together, they prepared two 8-seat tabletops and a 10-seat tabletop. That equaled 26 guests to feed and keep happy during dinner. Eva had neglected to mention one of the toughest things about their job: they had to memorize every order. Pencils and paper were not allowed.

She and Leon placed the designated meat plates with the blue flower design out first. Next, they put out the glasses. Finally, they added the cloth napkins and silverware. Familiar with kosher eating, she was careful not to mix *fleishigs* and *milkhik*. Meat and dairy were always served on separate plates and at separate meals. A meat or poultry dish would never include cream sauce. That was the reason they served café noir after dinner; you had to wait before the cream could be added. No pork or shellfish was ever part of any meal.

"It's time to gather the livestock," she overheard another waitress say as Leon finished placing the red wine and challah beside the Shabbat candlesticks in the center of the table.

On her way to the kitchen to collect the livestock, she paused to watch the busboys hustle across the elegant dining room. The livestock was the term for all the perishable food that the whole table shared. A real opportunity had been given to her, and she was ready to prove herself.

She grabbed the coleslaw first, followed by the

lemon slices, and marched forward. Leon held a small dish, commonly referred to as a monkey dish, that contained margarine. "Are you nervous?" he asked.

"I'm a bundle of nerves and excitement," she admitted.

Irving zipped by as she held a plate of pickles. "The guests will arrive soon, expecting every indulgence. The men wear jackets and ties, and the women are in fine dresses."

Once her boss was on the other side of the room, she snuck a pickle. The sweet, vinegary taste left her wanting more. She would have to stash an entire plate of pickles on her server stand for later.

Eva brushed by just before the guests poured in. She whispered, "Irving has eyes in the back of his head. He knows everything that goes on inside the dining room."

"Hello, I'm Dotty," she told the guests one by one since the Concord uniforms lacked nametags.

As soon as she turned to the next guest, the previous guest would ask the person beside them, "What do you do for a living?" It was always the first topic of discussion among tablemates.

The guests requested three and four of everything off the kosher menu. They wanted to get their money's worth. "There are five different varieties of herring offered!" one guest exclaimed.

"Sample them all," said another guest.

She dashed to the kitchen, loaded her round silver tray, held it high with her left hand, and pushed the door open with her right hand. Salads and assorted soups rested on her server stand beside the 10-top as she handed them out two at a time.

The last guest to receive his soup complained, "Why am I last? My matzo balls will be cold."

"You'll be the first to receive your entrée," she told him.

After a grunt, he seemed satisfied.

She went back to the kitchen for the entrées. Undoubtedly, her muscles would be much stronger by the end of summer.

She was picking up a plate of chicken when a guest hollered, "Where's a glass of milk?"

"I didn't realize there was a gentile at the table," Leon said to her.

"It's against the rules!" another guest yelled across the table.

The majority of guests were Jewish up in the mountains. The hotels catered to the Jewish population, offering a refuge since they were not welcome at most places. She found herself flabbergasted. *How could this person not know a goyish request for milk with meat was completely out of the question?*

In a matter-of-fact voice, Leon said, "Not until the meal is over. No *treif*. I'll bring you some juice instead."

The gentile guest crossed his arms. "I want the roast pork and garlic sandwich with a glass of milk."

"*Meshuga*," spat out another guest. "The entire menu is kosher."

The gentile guest accepted the juice Leon gave him without further complaint.

"I'll bring him some gefilte fish, carrot tzimmes, and kreplach, too," Dotty told Leon before asking another guest, "Would you like some coffee?"

"I haven't even had my juice yet!" shouted the guest.

She asked the next guest, "Would you like a cup of juice as well?"

That guest yelled, "I need my coffee first!"

She clenched her jaw, faking a smile and hoping Irving wasn't witnessing the outrage. But then she located him only tables away and threw her shoulders back over the lucky break. He was distracted by being in "King Cupid" mode, *schmoozing* with a young male guest and a young female guest.

Eva snuck up behind her and said, "Maybe Irving can orchestrate a courtship for you."

Her cheeks blushed. While making money was her biggest goal in the mountains, she would not mind ending up with a ring on her finger.

"Don't worry, it's your first day here." Eva pinched her arm. "You have plenty of time to meet a nice Jewish boy in the mountains. Say, do you want to go meet Hershel after we're done in here?"

Torn, she admitted, "My arms and legs ache."

Eva peered down her nose. "Only the strongest survive in the mountains."

"What luxury," Leon mumbled, removing a barely touched plate of boiled potatoes and setting it in his bus box. "Food rationing does not apply at the Concord."

Dotty waved goodbye to the final guest departing from her 10-top and stuffed a pickle into her mouth.

ABE

Abe tried to set the coffee cup down, but it would not balance on its own, and it kept sliding.

"Tsk tsk," said Eva. In a flash, she set a saucer underneath.

The guest *kvetched*. "Too cold."

"*Oy vey*," he muttered.

Eva whispered, "Run the cup handle under hot water until it's hot enough to satisfy her. It's a trick to make the guests believe their coffee is even hotter."

By the end of the meal, he heard the cold coffee complaint too many times to count.

Once the guests were gone, Eva said, "Nice job tonight."

He cleared the table with gusto, proud of the compliment, and ate the contraband stuffed pepper stashed at his station.

"After every meal, you have to exchange the linens," Eva explained. "The laundry attendant will count them all. It's not a problem getting supplies replenished; it's just a hassle."

He carried the tablecloths and cloth napkins to the linen room, conveniently located next to the kitchen. Always a gentleman, he offered to take over washing the silverware from Eva.

"Oh, Abe, you're a dear."

He rolled up his jacket sleeves, pushed his glasses further up his nose, and carried the silver bucket full of dirty silverware to the kitchen. While swishing it around and washing it with cold sink water, his final foster parents, to whom he credited all his gentlemanly traits, appeared in his thoughts. His foster father had led by example. He carried the silverware bucket out to Eva, where they dumped it onto a tablecloth.

"An entire roast chicken was thrown into the garbage," he said as they dried the silverware by shaking the tablecloth together.

Eva knitted her brows. "There's a ton of waste at the Concord."

Happy he would never feel hunger pains here; he would do his best not to create waste, which should not be a problem since eating was his favorite hobby. They sorted the cutlery.

"You did a terrific job tonight. Say, if you'd like to have a nightcap, swing by the Rio Cabana later." Eva twisted her heart-shaped necklace between her fingers.

A million-watt grin lit up his face. Even though he was spent and intent on a hot shower, the invitation intrigued and flattered him. He knew it was in his best interest to rub shoulders with the Rio Cabana crowd.

"The nightclub sits outside the main building. Bring your busboy friend over there." Eva jutted her jaw toward Leon as she turned to vacate the dining room.

Someone slapped him on his back. "I knew you would survive your first night," said Arthur Winarick.

Out of the corner of his eye, Abe saw Irving Cohen, mindful of the interaction. He stood a quarter of an inch taller and began to daydream, imagining himself as the maître d' in charge one day. He came to a swift understanding of how successful one could become in the rich resort industry that monopolized life up here. The biggest hotel owners had clout—they were driven, generous men with strong work ethics and major achievements.

Leon approached and punched him on the shoulder with a grin. "I saw Arthur over here."

"Don't be jealous; you'll get recognition in no time. Come with me; we've been invited to the nightclub."

"How'd that happen?" Leon asked with disbelief.

"Eva."

Leon rubbed his hands together. "Well, all right."

They marched outside. The full moon created a shimmering path that wrapped around hydrangea shrubs, ending at the Rio Cabana.

Abe's attention went straight to the stage, where a woman with poodle-like curls was belting out show tunes from *My Gal Sal*. To her left, a *tummler* was beating a drum set with his bare hands, and next to him, a musician played "Boogie Woogie" on the saxophone.

"*Shabbat Shalom*, fellas," bellowed a 6-foot-2-inch, muscular guy with a mop of pitch-black hair. He held a spiral-bound notepad in his left hand. "I'm Hershel. I book all the talent around here." He ran his eyes over them. "You must be working for Irving Cohen."

"We're busboys. Eva invited us," Abe said.

"I'm over here," Eva hollered from a corner table, waving a handful of cards.

"She's my poker shark." Hershel winked. "She has guests requesting her as their waitress from July 4th to Labor Day next season."

Abe tapped his feet to the beat of the music, overjoyed to be in such good company. A small gray cat with black stripes on its tail, wearing a thin yellow collar, slunk out of the shadows. Leon, who stood rigid with his lips pressed together, squatted down near the feline.

"We're celebrating, fellas." Hershel shook his notebook above his head. "I stole an act from Grossinger's—Danny Kaye was set to perform there. He'll be the headliner here that night instead!" Hershel did an impromptu jig and the cat rubbed against his leg. "Shoo, Boychik."

The cat meowed, swinging its tail back and forth.

"You know the deal. The Rio Cabana is your home as long as you control the country mouse population and stay out of the way," Hershel told the cat and reached for a bottle of Chivas.

"I heard Danny Kaye on the radio recently; he left me in stitches," Abe said.

"Not just anybody can make it on my stage," Hershel boasted. He set three glasses in a row. "It also helps that Winarick approves hefty payments for the entertainment." He winked again and poured two fingers of liquor into each glass.

Leon left his drink untouched on the bar and petted the cat while Abe finished his drink in one swallow. Three girls from the resident dance team sheathed in Roaring '20s flapper costumes pranced into the nightclub. Abe's pulse quickened watching the dresses glimmer around their thighs. The tallest one, with shiny brunette hair, cozied right up to Hershel. Pulling him into a flirty hug, the strap of her dress slid down her arm.

"Well, hello, dolly," Hershel said.

There was a ruckus as Eva stopped dealing cards.

Hershel looked as if he wanted to crawl between the pages of his notebook.

"Did you perform?" Leon asked a petite dancer with a bejeweled headband tucked around her dyed red hair. He held his drink now.

The dancer standing beside Hershel answered in a strong New Jersey accent. "Since it's the Sabbath, we practiced."

"We usually work 24 hours a day. It feels good to rest my feet," said a perky dancer with a rhinestone-feathered barrette. She had strawberry blonde hair.

Abe's pulse raced as he watched Eva swoop over and wrap her arms around Hershel. The New Jersey dancer turned her back to them, setting her eyes on the *tummler*.

The alcoholic beverages took effect. Leon was giving a foot massage to the dancer perched on the stool next to him. Hershel offered them more scotch. The strawberry blonde removed Abe's glasses and tickled his ear. Without his glasses, things became hazy.

A man in a charcoal fedora and a black trench coat burst through the door. The singer froze, the *tummler* clenched his fists, and the saxophonist almost lost his grip on the instrument.

"He's nefarious," Leon whispered over the sparkly headband.

Abe shoved his glasses back onto his face. "We must go," he whispered, eyeing the cat crouched with its back arched.

Leon conceded and slid off his stool.

"You have something that belongs to me," said the man dressed in head-to-toe black, piercing his eyes at Hershel.

The dancer who had taken a fancy to Abe stuck out her lower lip as he stealthily crept to the exit. Hershel faced the interloper, standing in a wide stance—he waved to the musicians to continue.

Abe eased the door shut behind them. A healthy distance away, near enough to the main hotel to make a run for it, he peeked over his shoulder. The glint from a moonbeam bounced off the mystery man's chunky brass pinky ring as he skulked out of the Rio Cabana. Abe kept his pace casual so as not to draw any unwanted attention their way.

Chapter 3
Week 1, Saturday

DOTTY

Dotty inhaled a plethora of fresh aromas wafting from the kitchen. She could not reach the coffee pot fast enough. It was common for the staff to stay out late partying and stampede in at the last possible second, guzzling caffeine as they prepared for the breakfast rush.

The smell of yeasty dough was intoxicating. Papa had said no European baker would use a pre-mixture of ingredients. That had been proven true. Everything was from scratch in the mountains.

Irving Cohen nodded at her in recognition of her prompt arrival. She was straightening a white tablecloth when Leon hoofed over. "Didn't you get any sleep?" She peered at the shadows under his eyes.

He blushed around his ears and balanced coffee cups in his arms. "After returning from the Rio Cabana, I managed a little. My roommate helped me regain my senses."

She followed his eyes toward the busboy assisting Eva. Abe looked just as sleepy. If she had known the busboys joined in the fun last night, she would have made more of an effort to stay awake. "Will you be playing poker tomorrow night?" She removed four of the cups stacked in Leon's arms and set them on the white-clothed table.

"I'm very much looking forward to it."

"Don't lose all your tips to Eva," she teased.

"We'll see about that." Leon's arms were empty

once again, and he pressed his hand against his pocket to shield it. "I hear she's a real poker shark."

A busboy from a neighboring station was stealing the coffee cups and saucers that she just set out. "Hey, you, stop!" she hollered.

He smirked, and she chased after him. Leon caught up to the thief of a busboy first, demanding that he hand over the stolen goods. With puppy dog eyes and a pouting lip, the busboy surrendered. Dotty shook her finger at him.

In a flurry, the coffee cups and saucers were back in their original place. Guests found their seats as she transformed into a cheerful waitress. She memorized orders and ran to the kitchen, focused straight ahead on her destination. Like a racing pony, she blocked others from her lane. She had seen those ponies at Coney Island with her papa that summer when they had rented a bungalow by the sea.

Back at her 8-top, she was holding her left arm high, balancing dishes with aluminum lids. An angry guest threw back his chair. Tomato juice was dripping down his shirt. *Oh, dear.* She set her tray on the stand.

"Where is that no-good busboy? Wait until I get my hands on him. I need a new shirt!" the guest yelled, lunging toward the exit.

Her hopes of a breeze, or even a good meal, diminished as she saw Irving sprint after the guest. She searched the dining room for Leon, worried about his well-being.

Eva keeled over in laughter. "That man went flying out the door like his pants were on fire."

"I'll offer to buy him a new shirt with my tip

money tomorrow night."

"Don't you dare. Arthur will give him a brand-new shirt—or maybe even two. It was an accident. Happens to all of us," Eva giggled.

Right on cue, Irving held a laundered shirt in the air. He presented it to the angry guest who'd raced back into the room in pursuit of Leon. The guest grumbled a list of distasteful words.

"I promise you'll get a good seat at Eddie Cantor's show tonight," said Irving.

The man swiftly took off his old shirt and replaced it with the new one, his face lighting up with a smile.

Dotty stood with a nervous expression, expecting a scolding from Irving. To her relief, he brushed by, intent on breaking up an argument between two guests on the other side of the room. That was that.

Leon resurfaced. "I didn't mean to, honest to God. It was an accident. I had to hide in the linen closet."

"You did the guest a favor. He got upgraded seats at Eddie Cantor's show."

Leon relaxed his shoulders. "I was afraid I might not live to see the show myself."

"Oh, we can't possibly miss Eddie Cantor," she squealed.

"Will your roommate be attending with you?"

"She wouldn't miss it, either."

Leon cleared dirty dishes clockwise with a jaunty step.

Dotty clucked her tongue at him. She was considering mentioning that Eva and Hershel were sweethearts. For now, she kept her mouth shut.

ABE

Abe gathered the disposable napkins used for breakfast and lunch. He had been dragging earlier. After two cups of coffee with two sugar cubes each, he was currently wide awake and ready for the lunch crowd. His mind kept flicking back to the night before with the dancers, and he could not hide his smile.

The guests buzzed with excitement in anticipation of Eddie Cantor's show later. They were also very hungry. A waitress placed the wrong order, and the chef chased after her with a meat cleaver. Abe stepped into the chef's path, intervening; the waitress blew him an air kiss over her shoulder. Eva was struggling with her tray. He went to help.

"I served a hundred monkey dishes of peaches and cream," Eva *kvetched*.

She was not kidding. He had been clearing and bringing stacks of the small bowls since the first guest sat down.

Once the midday meal was in the rearview mirror, he decided to take it easy during his 2:30 p.m. to 5:00 p.m. break. Friday night's dinner had taken a lot of energy. He was reserving some for tonight.

He had promised his younger sister Jean he would write to her, so he went to the sundry shop to buy a couple of postcards. The balding man with kind blue eyes behind the counter pointed at the standing rack. Abe was browsing the selection when another patron entered the shop; he wore a charcoal fedora, dark clothing, and a chunky brass pinky ring.

The man tipped his hat, reached for a bottle of

Jeris Hair Tonic, and pulled out a thick wad of cash. He peeled a bill off the top. "Keep the change."

"Win big." The shopkeeper winked and asked, "How long will you be a guest with us?"

"I'm booked until I'm handed over what belongs to me." The man cracked his knuckles and strode out of the shop.

Certain it was the same person from the Rio Cabana, Abe worried there would be trouble. A weekly rate was close to $75. He wondered how this fella afforded it and assumed there was some bootlegging involved. He eyed the shelf of Jeris, deciding he would buy a bottle after he collected his tips. "Must've been a heavy roller in here with that mighty generous tip."

The shopkeeper dropped his voice. "The heavy rollers are the best tippers." He glanced at the doorway. "It's wise to stay on their good sides."

Abe flashed a tight-lipped smile and picked out three postcards with F.D.R. outside of his Hyde Park house printed on the front.

"Who are you sending them to?" the shopkeeper asked as one of the six gold buttons on his navy blue vest came undone.

"My younger sister and my two brothers, who are in the Army." He pulled a coin from his pocket.

"I thank them for serving. Where are they stationed?" the shopkeeper asked while fastening the top button on his vest.

"Al, my eldest brother, has been in the Pacific for the last six months. He's a signal corps soldier, working as a communications specialist trained to focus on air operational elements. My youngest brother, Norman, was stateside, setting up anti-aircraft guns in Texas and California, but now, he's stationed in Europe." The shame of being safe at home while his brothers were not settled in his stomach.

"I will include them in my prayers," said the shopkeeper, without further questioning. He extended his hand. "I'm Marv. Anything you need, I have it here."

He returned the firm handshake and supposed a healthy living could be made by operating the sundry shop. Because the day was just as beautiful outside as on the picturesque postcard he selected, he found a spot near a patch of geraniums and irises in a rainbow of colors with Kiamesha Lake in view. For a moment, he fixed his gaze on a fishing boat paddling along the water. Then, he turned his attention to the stable across the street. Horses were trotting with guests riding in their saddles.

He wrote to Jean about the good life in the mountains, telling her everything was all-inclusive, and guests only needed their wallets for tipping. He underlined the sentence, explaining that it meant three meals a day, a long list of activities, and live entertainment. He also included the fact that he poured outrageous amounts of coffee every day. Jean was the baby of the family. His guilt over being released from active duty was strong, but the fact that Jean had a loving brother at home comforted him. It saved her from fearing that he would be harmed. She lived in Brighton Beach with Ma. That concerned him. Ma was selfish and had a sharp tongue. They all kept giving her second chances; she never failed to disappoint them.

Another time, he would write to Al and Norman about the kosher dining room mecca and the top entertainment. He tucked his pencil into his pocket and raised his head to see Arthur Winarick exiting his house on the hotel grounds. A security guard did a double take—not recognizing the big boss in his laid-back clothes right away. Abe chuckled into his hand. But his chuckles faded away, replaced by goosebumps. The man he had seen inside the sundry shop crept out of the hotel, clutching a gardening spade in his left hand.

DOTTY

Dotty intended to lie down between lunch and dinner. A door away from her own, she heard a male voice inside the room she shared with Eva. She tiptoed closer.

"There's a gangster up to no good lurking around. He claims half of the fortune belongs to him."

She heard a dresser drawer open and close before Eva asked, "Did you call *him*?"

"I'm trying, but it's not so easy to get someone on the phone who is sitting behind bars in prison."

The voices became even more hushed. She pressed her ear against the door.

"Baby, I buried it where nobody will find it. Between the apple trees and the chicken coop."

Buried what? She gulped and wobbled on her feet. Hearing nothing but silence now, she rubbed her ears.

Eva cried out. "That's the most obvious spot on the farm. You should have hidden it in a better location."

She pressed her ear back to the door, listening to Eva stomp in her Oxford heels.

"You have to hear back from *him*. I'm afraid they will tie you to a slot machine and throw you to the bottom of a lake if you don't follow their orders," said Eva, no longer stomping.

I think I'd better not eavesdrop anymore. Alarmed by the conversation, her curiosity was nonetheless piqued. Dotty went tiptoeing to the sundry shop.

"Welcome," said the balding man, wearing a snazzy vest behind the counter.

Once she stepped foot into the cozy shop, she let her guard down. It had always been her nature to lighten the mood. When she saw the Jeris Hair Tonic, she broke into the jingle. "Jeris hits the jackpot for greaseless good grooming and healthier, handsomer hair."

"Very good." The shopkeeper was clapping to the beat. "Nine out of 10 barbers use Jeris."

She curtsied and selected a postcard with a picture of the Concord on the front.

"Who are you sending it to?"

"My older sister, Selma. She's a secretary for the Manhattan Project."

"She must be very smart." He pointed at Dotty's waitressing uniform. "You must be very bright to work under Irving this summer."

She stood tall. The opportunity to succeed in the mountains was a gift. "I think I'm going to need those." She was pointing at a deck of playing cards sitting on the shelf.

"Have you had the pleasure of playing against Eva yet?"

"That's exactly why I must practice. Eva is

infamous around here, isn't she?" She slapped a coin onto the counter.

"Eva stole the heart of 'the Casanova of the Concord.' Have you met Hershel yet?"

She shook her head and opened her mouth to ask more about Hershel, but she was a second too late. A group of guests wanting reading material for the pool skipped into the shop. In the hallway, someone grabbed her hand. She fixed her gaze on the sheer tangerine scarf wrapped around the woman's head.

"I'm a *shadchante*," said the woman, studying her palm.

Caught off guard and a bit intrigued, she relaxed her hand. "Oh, what the heck."

The *shadchante* blinked three times. "I see a waiter in your future."

A lifeguard who saw the exchange wisely added, "Waitresses often fall for waiters."

The *shadchante* dropped Dotty's hand and wagged her finger at the lifeguard. He smirked and jogged away. Dotty shrugged her shoulders and went to find a spot to write her sister a note on the back of the postcard. She scribbled about sending Ma some money to buy a nice brisket for dinner as soon as she collected her tip money. Selma had been helping to support their parents financially, and she took pride in contributing as well.

Unsure if enough time had passed, she headed back to her room at the Colonial anyway, hoping to find it empty.

"What in the world?" she said aloud as she picked up a crumpled newspaper article off the ground. She

flattened it, and the date showed May 5 in the corner.
Murder, Inc.'s Jacob "Jack" Drucker, Convicted of Second-Degree Murder, Gets 25 Years to Life.

Having only heard Jack Drucker's name spoken in vile tones, a chill slithered up her spine after reading the headline. She did not know his specific rap sheet but knew of Murder, Inc.'s sinister reputation. Last March, Papa told her the gangsters' reign of power had officially ended following the executions of Lepke Buchalter, Louis Capone, and Mendy Weiss. Fearful that Papa had been wrong, she stuffed the newspaper article under her pillow. Then she threw the curtains open and waited for Eva to return.

Chapter 4

Irving intercepted Abe and Leon as soon as they entered the dining room. "You're both assigned to two waitresses tonight during dinner."

Abe shook Irving's hand. "I was comfortable bussing for one waitress, so what's another one added to the mix?"

"It's the most talented busboys who carry six tables." Irving shook Leon's hand and pointed to the left corner. He turned back to Abe and pointed to Eva and Dotty.

"Now we'll have more money in our pockets for the Sunday night poker game. Do you want to switch stations?" Leon asked, hopeful.

"That might upset Irving. One day you'll get paired with Eva's tables." He sensed Leon was sweet on Eva.

It was double the work, hustling around helping two waitresses prepare their stations. Abe stepped back and admired the splendid setting. Guests waltzed into the dining room in their ornate dresses and tailored suits.

At the meal's end, Dotty spun around with a coffee pot as he carried his overflowing bus box to the kitchen. Leftover prime rib spilled onto his white bussing jacket.

"Oh, I'm so sorry," Dotty said.

"At least it wasn't a guest wearing his or her mandated dinner attire," he said.

She dabbed at the stain with a napkin, spreading it around into a bigger mess.

"I'll drop it off for laundering as soon as the guests head to the show. They'll be shouting about cold coffee soon enough. Go." He shooed her away.

It seemed like an eternity before they cleared all the plates, dried the silverware, and he was able to slip out of his soiled jacket. Leon caught up to him. "It was difficult work tonight."

"You aren't kidding." He headed straight to the shower. The water helped rejuvenate him. Before he knew it, Leon was shouting that they should leave for the show. He toweled off and dressed in a hurry.

Pushing through the doors of the Rio Cabana, Leon said, "It's almost curtain time."

Abe scooted to the side to let a group of middle-aged women dressed in mink stoles hustle past.

"I don't want anyone to trample me," Leon said.

Some guests faked boredom; others were on the edge of their seats, waiting for the dance routine and the much-anticipated comedian. Arthur Winarick and his wife, Jeanie, tucked themselves into a spot front and center.

Cocktail waitresses were trying to get people to order alcoholic beverages before the first act. A guest flung a wrist in irritation at the suggestion to order a cocktail. "I'll take water."

"Look, there's Hershel." Abe waved to him as if they had been friends forever and puffed out his chest like a big shot. They cut through the crowd.

"Welcome, fellas." Hershel greeted them each with a slap on the back. He kept his spiral-bound notebook wedged under his arm the entire time. Eva positioned herself in the crook of Hershel's other arm.

Abe watched Leon stiffen his posture. The little gray cat was hovering in the background.

"Nice job assisting two waitresses tonight. I overheard Irving calling you two firecrackers. You'll be waiters in no time at this rate." Hershel winked.

Abe beamed. He would love to advance and fill his pockets even more.

"Irving was a busboy over at Grossinger's. Then he became a waiter here in the late '30s and worked his way up to maître d'," said Eva.

"There's no reason to be at the G when you can be at the Concord. I booked George Burns and Gracie Allen for next month," Hershel said.

"Their 'Dumb Dora' act is very funny. I loved them in *A Damsel in Distress*, and I enjoy listening to *The Burns and Allen Show* on the radio," Eva squealed.

Curious to know why Hershel and Irving were not off to war, Abe went ahead and asked.

Hershel flexed his muscles. "Irving's on the civil defense, but I'm just as mighty, I assure you."

His eyes widened. He knew being on the civil defense meant you were one of the strongest in the community. The cat, too, was impressed, as it chose to pounce out of the shadows at that moment.

Hershel ignored the cat and continued. "The war broke out, and my three brothers and I took over our father's farm to avoid the draft. We supply the Concord with eggs and milk. I didn't want to spend all day in the barn, but I'm still a partner."

A cocktail waitress, batting her eyes, paused with a hand on her hip. Hershel pointed at Abe and Leon. "Bring us a round of scotch. And an orange blossom cocktail for my gal." The cat rubbed against Hershel's legs. "Shoo, Boychik."

The cat meowed again.

"You're probably wondering how I made the leap to on-site talent booker. Well, I'll tell you. I was a waiter for Winarick one summer, and I kept complaining about the entertainment. So I told him I could do a better job, and he put me up to the challenge. I organized one hell of a show! The staff in the dining room were part of it. I scored the job!"

"Most of the hotels use the acclaimed talent bookers on West 46th Street in Manhattan—Beckman and Pransky," Eva said.

"A lot are going with Charlie Rapp now," said Hershel.

"Hershel is a jack-of-all-trades. Not only does he book all the talent, but he acts as a bouncer if needed," Eva said.

Hershel flexed his muscles again and nudged the cat away with his foot. "I'll take care of you if you run into trouble. I've been known to threaten people who don't settle their gambling debts. If you see someone whisper in my ear and I rush off, I'm going to the parking lot to collect the money. Don't hesitate to use my services if you need me. I throw a powerful knuckle sandwich."

Hershel would definitely be the first person he would seek if he ever got himself in a quandary. As for Leon, standing off to the side now petting a purring Boychik, his body language portrayed distrust.

Hershel leaned in. "I did Irving's dirty work all winter. I'd call the G to see if they had vacancies. If they sold out, we knew the Concord would receive the overflow. The Concord wasn't a smashing success from day one, you see. The competition is tough in the mountains."

The cocktail waitress returned with a full tray of drinks. Hershel winked. "Since I've been managing the shows, the Concord has developed its own clientele."

Abe tasted the scotch and waved Leon to his side. They clinked glasses before gulping the drinks down.

"Attaboy." Hershel slapped him on the back first and Leon second.

"This is Dotty," Eva told Hershel before taking a generous sip of her orange blossom cocktail.

Abe nodded hello to her.

"It's a pleasure to meet you, Dotty." Hershel crinkled his eyes and flipped a page in his notebook. "I'm a man in demand."

Eva stood on her toes and gave him a peck on the cheek. Abe watched Leon's jaw muscle tighten.

"Come on, Dotty, let's use the powder room before the show," said Eva.

"Enjoy yourself, fellas." Hershel bounded away.

The lights in the club dimmed, and the dancing act frolicked on stage. "Well, I'll be," said Leon, waving his hand in the air at the red-haired dancer.

"A moment ago, I thought it was Eva you were sweet on."

Leon cupped a hand over his ear. Abe mouthed, "Never mind." The strawberry-blonde dancer in her black fringed dress was irresistible. He was having a jolly good time.

The act garnered lots of applause, then the lights

illuminated the stage. Eddie Cantor glided to the center, performing a skit with his signature eye-rolling.

"They don't call him 'Banjo Eyes' for nothing," Leon said.

He laughed hard and tried to remember a couple of jokes to include in the next postcard he would write to Jean. The crowd was wild—they wanted more entertainment, more Eddie Cantor.

Once the stage lights went dark, he searched the nightclub, hoping to spot the dancers from the previous night. Instead, one of the mink-stole-wearing women from earlier found him. "What are you gentlemen doing for the rest of the evening? Our husbands are in the city, and we'd like to have a good time."

Hershel elbowed him. "Why not go show them a good time?"

The woman wearing an ivory stole and gaudy earrings stepped forward. "The night is young."

"We have a 'staff-only' poker game to get to," he fibbed, pivoting before he dashed away.

"You'll be a night early," Hershel cackled.

He turned to Dotty, the closest person in his proximity. "Would you like to dance?"

DOTTY

"Oh, Eddie Cantor was so funny," Dotty said, thrilled that the first show she saw in the mountains was such a big name.

"He sure was entertaining," Eva agreed. "One day we'll be telling our grandkids all about these acts."

Someone tapped on her right arm; she spun around and came face to face with Abe the busboy.

"Would you like to dance?" he asked.

Without missing a beat, she followed him to the area in front of the bandstand. The Latin band started their set. She wiggled her hips and tapped her feet in harmony. At first, there was about a foot of space between them. As the songs continued, they inched closer. Their feet touched, then their shoulders. Oh, what fun she was having with a handsome busboy. Butterflies fluttered in her stomach as the *Concord Evening News* photographer knelt before them and angled his camera upward.

During the band's break, Abe said, "I think it's safe to return to our friends." Then he excused himself to use the washroom as she joined Eva.

"You two cut a rug out there," said Hershel.

She would not have minded dancing the night away. Hearing Hershel's voice, she knew he had been the voice behind the door talking with Eva earlier. Right now, though, she was too excited about the current happenings to focus on the angst she had overheard.

Eva winked at her and then said with a playful tone, "I hear Jack Benny is over at Grossinger's." Hershel balled his hands into fists and shook his notebook in the air. "His act with the violin is funny," Eva continued to kid.

"Baby, I ought to throw you out on the curb." Hershel pinched Eva with a playful grin.

Eva batted him away. "*Oy vey,* there would be too much traffic, anyway."

Hershel bent down, kissed Eva on the lips, and fixed her opal heart necklace so it rested at the nape of her neck. A pang of envy shot through Dotty.

"Why don't you dance some more with Abe? Unless he's busy." Hershel's gaze was straight ahead, and a smile teased his lips.

She blushed and followed Hershel's line of vision. A group of women in mink stoles circled Abe and Leon.

"They sure do want to have a good time without their husbands." Hershel waved his notebook in the air and darted off.

Eva told her, "Don't wait up for me," and chased after him.

She stood alone and listened to a conversation beside her.

"I saw Hershel necking with the head camp counselor on the volleyball court not too long ago."

"Everyone knows all the guys are gaga for the day camp counselors."

"Eva is such a pretty little thing. She should find herself a different fella."

Dotty pursed her lips and squinted at Hershel. She intended to ask Eva about the newspaper clipping and Jack Drucker real soon. She also intended to say farewell to Abe and Leon, but with them nowhere in sight, she departed the Rio Cabana solo. Lost in her thoughts, a man blended into the darkness so well that if not for the wind picking up and blowing his fedora from his head, she would have missed him altogether. She doubled her pace, wishing the clouds would unblock the waning moon from lighting her path home.

Chapter 5
Week 1, Sunday

ABE

Abe charged over to Eva's 8-top during lunch. He was holding two monkey dishes; then he shifted his attention to Dotty's 10-top, where most of the seats were occupied. He caught her eye, mouthing he would be over to help shortly. Loose-limbed due to his full night of sleep, he and Leon had successfully locked themselves in their room. It had been the safest bet to avoid the mink stole-wearing women intent on seducing them.

Slack-jawed over how fast the guests were slurping down their cold borscht and tuna fish sandwiches while others seemed to have a lighter appetite than usual, Eva explained to him, "They want to go back to their rooms and pack. The dining room will clear out right after lunch."

"We've got to beat the traffic," said the father of two sitting at Eva's 8-top.

"We were stuck behind a Ford truck that ran out of gas in Rock Hill the last time. It blocked traffic for hours. We don't want that to happen again," said his wife.

"Can you hurry me a plate of boneless sardines?" the father asked.

Abe flew through the kitchen. His ears perked up when he overheard the steward tell the salad man, "A waitress broke her ankle. Irving will be short on help this weekend."

With a bounce in his step, he pictured more coins

in his pockets as he slid the plate of sardines in front of the guest. A pang of concern over the competition shot through him. His chances were likely lower than Leon's since he was not a refugee. Everyone at Eva's tables seemed content, so he hustled back to Dotty.

"Ready to collect your first set of tips?" she whispered.

"I sure am." There was a twinkle in his eye.

The first guest, anxious to rush out the door, gave Dotty some cash. The same guest then turned to him and handed him half that amount. The routine was repeated at Eva's tables.

"We did well," Dotty said once the dining room was empty of all guests.

"We sure did." He shook his hands above his head and watched her wiggle her hips, doing an informal little dance. She had been a fun partner the night before. Perhaps he would ask her out dancing again sometime.

Another busboy galloped by and shouted about being stiffed. He considered joining him in pursuit of the tawdry guest, but he saw Arthur Winarick re-enter the dining room and decided to stay put.

"Hello, Abe," said Arthur.

The busboy returned from the parking lot, waving a bundle of money. Arthur grimaced and went to speak to him.

Sneaking up from behind, Dotty squealed, "You're making an impression."

He stood there grinning over being on a first-name basis with the owner until he saw Eva pulling the tablecloth off her 10-top. He hopped into cleanup mode.

Eva placed the dirty linens into his arms. "You must be happy with your tips."

"I hope every week is like this!"

"Become a waiter and you will have even better weeks."

En route to drop the linens off at the laundry room, he saw another busboy pull five pounds of Nova lox out of his pants.

"Irving has X-ray vision. Be careful not to follow his lead," Leon warned.

Once he returned to their station, Eva said, "I have to plan for the game tonight."

"Go, I can finish up," he motioned his hand toward the exit.

Leon scampered out the door, too.

Hershel came striding into the dining room. "Where's Eva?"

"She went to practice for the poker game later."

"I was going to take her for an egg cream. Come, I have a top-notch cigar to share with you inside the Rio Cabana instead."

In the hectic lobby, he saw guests leaving with jars of pickled herring as a memento. Other guests were arriving and checking in. A bellhop pushed a wardrobe filled with brightly colored clothing. Abe turned to his colleague and joked, "I wish I'd worn my sunglasses because the clothes are so flashy."

Even the guests let out a chuckle. Boychik shot through the lobby.

"Cats don't belong here. Scram!" the bellhop yelled. He let go of the cart to chase Boychik.

Abe grabbed hold of the cart before it rolled over a guest's foot. He kept his eyes on Boychik, who ran down the entire length of the check-in desk, knocking over a vase of flowers as he slid into a cup of pens, which spilled on the ground. The bellhop lunged over the desk, grabbing for Boychik's tail, missing entirely and landing flat on his face. Hershel raised his eyes to the ceiling, pretending not to know the animal.

Arthur Winarick arrived on the scene. He helped the bellhop to his feet. "What's going on here?" the big boss asked.

A guest pulled a "for later" roll out of her purse. "Here, kitty, kitty."

Boychik showed no interest in the bread roll and darted outside. Arthur Winarick stood shaking his head and threw his hands into the air. "I hope you enjoyed your first show here," he joked to the guests checking in.

Guests clapped while Abe gave the cart back to the bellhop. He and Hershel continued to the empty nightclub.

He was now enjoying a relaxed moment near the bar. Boychik, after his wild sprint, was resting on a stool next to him. Hershel lit the cigar and shooed the cat away. "You've caused enough trouble already."

Boychik looked up at Hershel and meowed as he jumped off the stool.

The click-clack of high heels on the hard floor echoed throughout the nightclub. "Hi, Hershy," the dancer with the New Jersey accent giggled.

Hershel rested the cigar in the ashtray and opened a bottle of Chivas.

The strawberry blonde click-clacked her way to Abe's side, tousling his hair and giggling in his ear. "Remember me? Fran, the dancer."

He assured her that she was unforgettable and ogled her floral print, turn-down collar dress. The Chivas slid right down his throat.

The red-haired dancer stood with her left hand on her hip and asked, "Where's your other pal?"

Hershel had a goofy grin on his face. "Not here, but the two of us are." He leaned in toward Abe and said, "If Eva hears I've been spending time with the dance team, I'm a dead man."

"You have my word; I won't say a thing." He lost count of how many fingers of scotch Hershel consumed as he watched two dancers twirl in front of him. He, on the other hand, had to stay sober enough to get through dinner.

DOTTY

Eva shook the latest issue of the *Concord Evening News* at Dotty. "It's straight off the press."

The black and white photograph taken inside the Rio Cabana made her entire body blush. She and Abe's inclusion in the calendar of events and gossipy content was astounding.

"Abe's a real dreamboat. You should sit next to him tonight at the poker game." Eva winked.

She blushed again. Now was the perfect time to ask about the Drucker business. Just as she reached under her pillow for the newspaper article, there were three swift knocks on the door.

Eva swung it open to find Leon. "What brings you by?"

He coughed into his right hand. "Would you be able to teach me tricks for waiting tables?"

Eva wagged her finger at him. "So, you want more coins in your pocket. Stick around once the poker game ends."

After a bunch of thank-you's, Leon left.

"Maybe Abe will ask you to teach him tricks." Eva winked at her again. "I'm going to go see Hershel before dinner."

Eva ran out the door, and she stuffed the clipping under her pillow. She changed into her white uniform and fussed with her hair before departing for the next meal.

"Hershel is a *zhlub*." Eva brushed right by, lumbering into the dining room.

Dotty stood back. She had already learned it was wise to give Eva her space with the mood she was in. The setup flew by. A woman who looked like she had been on a strict diet for decades was at her 10-top, making demands. "I want a boneless carp filet and a tossed salad with mixed greens tonight. That's it."

"What about soup?"

The woman swatted both her hands through the air. "No bread, either."

All the hotels expected the salad men to be artistic. She went to speak with him.

The picky woman received her salad, stabbed her fork into a bed of iceberg lettuce, took a bite, and frowned. She pushed her plate away. "I'm done."

During dessert, as Dotty was fetching honey cake, Eva hurried to her side and said, "It's almost poker time." Then she wrinkled her nose at a man who gently tucked a curl behind a woman's ear. "The last couple at my station is content to chat the breeze over coffee and halva."

About an hour later, Dotty settled around the poker table they had moved outside of the Colonial. She held a copy of the *Concord Evening News*. The seat to the right of her remained empty until Eva directed Abe to claim it.

"Hello, Dot," said Abe. He swatted at a mosquito.

"Did you see our picture?" She turned to page four and handed the hokey paper to him.

"Well, isn't that something? I'll have to save a copy for my sister. She'll get a real kick out of it."

"Where's Hershel?" asked Leon.

"Abe can tell you he's otherwise entertained by a certain dancer." Eva shot Abe a death stare and dealt the deck with a vengeance.

Abe fidgeted in his seat.

"I've been known to beat Eva once in a blue moon, and right now, I'm feeling lucky." The chef cracked his knuckles.

Eva declared, "Let's play."

Smiling at the pair of jacks in her hand, she would try for three of a kind. Ma would be proud. She lost herself in the action until a straight was tossed onto the table, and Eva bounced out of her seat.

Dotty raised her hand over her mouth. Abe slapped his thigh. Eva scooped her money into her hands and said, "I win a lot."

"You were hoping for some beginner's luck, weren't you? Eva is that damn good." The chef took a swig from his flask.

The next game got underway, and the table applauded Leon as he threw down four of a kind and won the hand. Eva cheered as well, although Dotty detected a scowl underneath her goodwill.

While they were putting away the cards, Abe said, "If I win next time, I'll take you out for an egg cream."

Butterflies flapped in her belly for a moment until she saw Eva pretending to hoist a tray in the air, with Leon watching her every move.

"What are they up to?" Abe asked.

"Leon's full of ambition," she said.

Abe narrowed his eyes. "I'm beat."

It was on the tip of her tongue to ask why Eva had been so cold toward him as they walked side by side inside the Colonial. She watched him yawn once, yawn again, and again. Since he was on the verge of exhaustion, she canceled the interrogation. Instead, she said, "I'm going to recount my tips. Good night."

"Good night, Dot."

She pictured herself winning the poker game after her pockets were already overflowing with tips, like Eva. In her room, she was humming with glee, stuffing her hard-earned money under the mattress when the doorknob turned.

Eva called over her shoulder, "Always put a smile on your face. Big smiles can mean big tips."

"Thank you for the invaluable lessons," Leon said, his voice expressing sincerity from the hallway.

She reached under her pillow and pulled out the newspaper clipping as the door clicked shut and Eva plopped face down on her bed. "Are you all right?"

Eva did not lift her head from the pillow. This time, Dotty placed the article on the set of drawers next to her. Tomorrow would be the day she got some answers.

Around midnight, the sound of the door opening and shutting jolted her out of a dream. She rolled over and peeked out of one eye at the empty bed on the opposite side of the room. *Where did Eva go?*

CHAPTER 6
Week 1, Thursday

ABE

Abe whistled a joyful tune. He had been bussing the tables for the same guests since Monday. As he removed a plate of jelly danishes, a woman with wrinkly hands squeezed his right cheek. "Would you like to go out dancing?" she asked in a gravelly voice.

"I think Irving needs me," he fibbed, pressing a palm to his stinging cheek. He scooted toward his boss, who was holding an empty plate in the air and waving it around in front of Arthur Winarick.

"Boy, that labor union captain is persistent. If I get my hands on him, I'll show him who is the boss around here."

"You have my word, Irving. No union is coming to the Concord," Arthur said.

Abe braced for a plate to smash on the ground, but Irving seemed satisfied with Arthur's promise. He simply set the dishware on the closest server stand.

Arthur nodded at him. "I trust you won't be attending the meeting about a union at the Concord."

"No, sir." If Irving and Arthur were against unions, he was, too.

"If any of your co-workers are considering attending, advise them not to."

"Sure thing." He wanted to ask Arthur to recommend him to Irving for the waiter job, but he worried it might make him seem like a bootlicker. He decided against it.

About midway through breakfast, he spilled

prune juice on his jacket. He wiped it off as best he could. Eva brushed by and hissed, "Wild night with the dance team?"

His eyebrows rose a notch.

After the meal, Leon and Irving were in a huddle. An idea popped into his mind. It was rather manipulative but might work in his favor. Lost in thought as he stepped into the sunshine, a bellhop approached him. "Your mother rang you through the hotel switchboard."

He followed the bellhop to the front desk.

"Abe-*ala*, Jean, and I are coming to the Concord for the week. Max has business in Pittsburgh. We want the nicest room."

He scratched his head; *this was not such a great idea. Ma had a way of bringing turmoil everywhere she went.* "All the rooms are nice, Ma. I don't assign them."

"Max is footing the bill, so I expect to be bathed in luxury. We'll be there by dinnertime."

His wealthy stepfather, Max, always gave Ma what she wanted. If not, Ma complained endlessly. He remembered when he was around six years old and Ma went missing. They all assumed she was at the 5&10 admiring the gold and silver trinkets; she always loved pretty things. Upon her return, she wore a brand-new mink stole paired with a black beaded purse and told them she had been at the theater with a man named Potamkin.

"Potamkin would want you to have the best," he said, not realizing his error.

"Why are you bringing up that old *paskudnyak*?" Ma spat into the phone.

"Max, I mean Max," he said. The unusual name had stuck since that was the man Ma had run off to Chicago with, abandoning four kids along the way. He said goodbye and jogged back to the Colonial, already pitying whoever had to serve Ma her meals. At least Jean was always pleasant and did a good job deflecting Ma's sourpuss attitude.

When he returned to their room, Leon waved his pencil hello and continued writing a letter. Abe considered getting the ball rolling on his plan. However, since Leon was probably corresponding with a refugee, his guilt became too heavy to proceed. He just stretched out on his bed.

DOTTY

Dotty was itching to get out of her uniform; potato pudding and fruit sherbet had spilled down the front of it. She deserved that for laughing at Abe for spilling prune juice on his jacket at breakfast. Unlike busboys' jackets, it was the waitresses' responsibility to get their dresses laundered.

After lunch, she heard the head chef ask Abe and Leon, "So, whose last week of bussing tables is it? There's one position open."

The chef was enjoying the uncomfortable situation; she was not and fled.

A lovely rendition of "I Left My Sugar Standing in the Rain" performed by a guest in the lobby made her forget her urgent desire to change out of her dirty uniform. She swayed to the tune. Jeanie Winarick was being serenaded by the singer.

Once she slipped into casual clothing, she scrubbed at the stains on her uniform until they were nonexistent. A Lucky Strike was her reward. She took a drag and blew a ring of smoke before writing a letter home. If it were possible to send a cool breeze from the mountains to her family's apartment in the Bronx, she would have sealed it inside the envelope.

Just as she put the pencil to paper, Eva returned, and Dotty did not waste any time waving around the newspaper clipping. Eva snatched it out of her hand, "Come on. I'm taking you *yagde* picking. I know the perfect spot by the lake where I'll explain."

She trooped after Eva into the day which seemed to have a split personality. Earlier, she had opened her eyes to brilliant saffron beams of sunlight; an hour later, a rain shower threatened to halt all outdoor activities. Now the sun was back. She gazed out at the lake, eager for Eva to start the conversation.

"There's nothing as delightful as a *yagde* warmed by the sun." Eva crouched down and picked ripe blueberries off the bush. "Do you think Irving will choose Leon or Abe to become a waiter?" In the same breath, she continued, "I'd choose Leon," and then ate all the fruit in her hand.

Dotty reached for a blueberry and popped it into her mouth.

Eva gently touched the gold chain with the opal-shaped heart she always wore around her neck. "This necklace was given to me by one of the first guests I ever served dinner to right here at the Concord. I was bone tired, unaware of how strenuous working in the dining room would be. There was a pompous *alta cocker* badgering me to join him at the casino. There was also this little old lady named Sally sitting at one of my tables. She reminded me of my British grandmother. Once I was done with my duties, she insisted I play poker with her. When I picked up my cards, my exhaustion completely disappeared. That's how my love of poker began."

Dotty scooted closer, inspecting the opal. The hand-cut gemstone's breathtaking hues of red, pink, purple, and aquamarine sparkled in the sunshine.

"I've worn the necklace ever since. At the time, I didn't know Sally was spending her last vacation at the Concord. She passed away from a long-term illness a week after that trip."

Dotty placed her hand over her heart.

Eva picked a handful of blueberries and blurted out, "Abe was there, fraternizing with the dance team. I saw him inside the Rio Cabana when I went to tell Hershel good night."

She stopped admiring the necklace to imagine the scene. She had woken up every morning looking forward to bantering with Abe throughout the day. How foolish.

"I should teach Hershel a lesson and find a new *bashert*, especially now with all the funny business with gangsters." Eva trailed off and plopped onto the ground.

After brushing away dirt with her shoes, Dotty sat next to her. Eva stared at a rowboat drifting by. "Are you familiar with Murder, Inc.?"

She nodded and crushed a blueberry between her fingers.

"It officially dissolved once the Brooklyn District Attorney got involved, but don't be fooled into thinking that no associates remain. Pay attention and you'll start to notice one sneaking around."

Pulling her knees into her chest, she pictured the man she had seen outside of the Rio Cabana after Eddie Cantor's show.

Eva cleared her throat. "How about the name Jack Drucker?"

She nodded again and spoke up. "I read the article. He's recently been sent to prison for murder."

"That's correct. Drucker was the chief of Murder, Inc.'s Sullivan County branch. He's the one 'certain people' turned to when they wanted the elimination of a disloyal henchman or a witness suspected of squealing. He also ran one of the most lucrative and profitable gambling rackets in the mountains. The feds found slot machines all over the hotels and bungalow colonies." Eva paused to pop a blueberry into her mouth. "He owns the farm next to Hershel's. They are well acquainted, unfortunately."

She was going to ask about the funny business when Hershel came bounding over to them. Eva's face turned into a sneer.

"Baby, I've been searching all over the hotel for you."

"The dance team must be busy."

"Baby." Hershel squirmed. "I have something important to discuss."

Eva put her hands on her hips and glared.

Hershel coughed a little. "It's a private matter."

"I have to get back to the Colonial, anyway." Dotty hurried away and stubbed her toe. Pain shot through her foot. She squatted near white hydrangeas and was still within eavesdropping range.

Hershel said, "I received word from the Attica prison."

Eva gave a high-pitched cry of surprise.

Dotty limped into the hotel, her curiosity through the roof.

Chapter 7

ABE

A bellhop hollered through the door of the Colonial for Abe, and his stomach twisted. There was always fear while his brothers were off at war that bad news would come.

"Somebody is asking for you in the lobby."

There was no way Ma and Jean could have traveled that fast. He hurried after the bellhop.

A man carrying a briefcase and a piece of paper almost bumped into him. Abe snatched the paper out of his hands, stuck it in his back pocket, and rushed to the lobby. His stomach dropped to his toes when he saw all 5 feet 3 inches of Papa standing before him.

"My son!" Papa called out. His eyes crinkled, and his arms were held out wide.

"Is something wrong, Papa? Why are you in the mountains?"

"I wanted to surprise my son who's just a bus ride away." Papa wrapped his arms around him and whispered into his ear, "I'm proud of you. Who knew you'd land in such a palace?"

He scoured the room.

Papa kept his voice low. "Minnie isn't here."

Still, he stepped back to check all corners for his rotten stepmother.

"I came alone."

He scratched his ear, wishing his two brothers were here as witnesses. Minnie always kept Papa on such a tight leash. They would not believe it. They would think they were hearing tall tales. "Did you ditch Minnie for once?"

Papa picked up his worn tweed bag. "It's true, son. I booked a stay through the weekend."

With a warm heart, he nudged his father out of the way and hooked the suitcase handle in his fist. He might skip for joy over the fact that Minnie stayed home, but then he stopped dead in his tracks. If he opened his mouth to tell Papa that Ma was on her way, it would ruin the cheerful mood. He snapped his jaw shut and led Papa through the hallway.

"Did you bring a nice jacket for the Friday and Saturday dinners?"

"Yes. I only recently got rid of my old one with the brown buttons."

The mention of that jacket caused him to fall into a long-ago memory. It was of Papa, at a graveside in Philadelphia, wearing that jacket and reciting *bruchas* for the recently deceased. He and his brothers had watched the scene from behind a tree, making themselves scarce. They were proud of Papa after the ceremony because he had a coin or two in his pocket.

At their destination, Papa jammed his room key into the lock. "My own room."

"A couple of nights away from Minnie in the mountains will be good for you."

Papa balanced on the corner of his mattress, tenderness in his eyes. "I've always felt guilty for the way my marriage to Minnie affected my *kinder*."

Abe flicked on a lamp. He could not recall the last time he had been in his stepmother's presence. She never encouraged any sort of relationship with her stepchildren.

"Before Minnie came into the picture, you all

relied on me to visit every Sunday, and without fail, I did. Whatever foster home you and your siblings were living in, and often with no carfare, I'd walk from one end of Philadelphia to the other to see my *kinder* for a couple of hours." Papa had tears in his eyes.

"The adventures you took us on were the highlight of our weeks."

"The afternoons we spent together at the Franklin Institute and Betsy Ross's home were special," Papa said, wiping his eyes with the back of his hand.

"My favorite trips were to Fairmount Park. There would be all those picnic blankets with homemade goodies."

"They represented Eastern European *shtetls*. You and your brothers would go straight for the frankfurters, and Jean always wanted a slice of watermelon."

The happiness on the days Papa visited with a nickel for each of them filled his heart once again.

"I should never have stopped my weekly Sunday visits." Papa bowed his head into his hands.

He seized the opportunity to ask Papa a question he had been wanting to ask for ages. "Why did you marry such an unpleasant woman?"

"Because I couldn't fight her any longer, Minnie's first husband left her for another woman, so she feels she must hold on even tighter to me."

"I can't blame the first one for bailing." He pitied Papa. "Do you remember when you introduced Minnie to us? She couldn't sit down on any furniture until she tore off her corset."

Papa kneaded his hands together. "You *kinder* were living in the final foster home. I knew you wanted frankfurters and all I gave you was a stern-mannered woman who made a spectacle of herself and bossed you around."

"You're here now, Papa, and there's a lot more on the menu than frankfurters." He realized that he needed to speak with Irving right away about seating Papa at the farthest table on the opposite side of the room from Ma. His stomach was a ball of unease over his parents being under the same roof. "Take a rest, Papa."

As he headed to talk to Irving, he removed the paper from his back pocket. He unfolded it and read over a couple of sentences. It was kismet when he bumped right into Leon.

"Say, Leon, I hear there's a union meeting going on right now. Are you going?" He ignored all guilt.

"A union, huh? I don't know much about any of that."

"Well, that's all the more reason to attend. It says right here you'll get to meet the union captain in person." He handed the piece of paper over.

"All right, I'll go with you."

He paused and scratched his ear. "I can't go because my papa showed up."

"Isn't your ma coming to visit?"

"She's on her way."

Leon's eyes bugged out of his head. "You don't say! I'll report back with everything I learn at the meeting."

His deceit sat heavy in his stomach, but he had no time to dwell on it. He had to find Irving before Ma's hack spit her out at the Concord gates. He sprinted to his boss's office.

DOTTY

Back in the room, Dotty was hoping Eva would return and pick right up where she left off; instead, Leon inched the door open. He held a piece of paper out to her. "Might you and Eva want to attend? Abe isn't able to because his papa arrived unexpectedly. It says the meeting starts right now. I'd better get a move on it."

"Wait, I'll come with you. I don't know much about unions. Eva is with Hershel. It'll just be me." She dabbed scarlet-colored lipstick onto her lips and spritzed perfume onto her wrists.

Leon folded the paper in half and led the way. She took a sharp breath.

Irving was standing with his arms crossed and his eyebrows furrowed in front of the doorway to the solarium. "What are you two doing here?"

"We have this flyer, Boss." Leon showed it to him.

Irving yanked the piece of paper out of Leon's hands and balled it into his fist. "I forbid any of my staff to entertain this nonsense. And I refuse to be beholden to gangsters."

She stood without flinching, even though she wanted to hide behind the curtains.

"If you are interested in a labor union, find another job," Irving said, his face reddening.

Leon stammered, "We were going to stick our heads inside and stay for a minute at the most."

Two men emerged, walking quickly. "Good evening," they said, tipping their fedoras.

She swallowed hard. The one on the left was the

nefarious man she had seen outside the Rio Cabana after Eddie Cantor's show. It seemed likely he was the associate of Murder, Inc. that Eva had mentioned.

"The Concord doesn't need unions with *shtarker* ties," spat Irving. "Intimidation and corruption don't work on me. You aren't going to take workers' dues for personal luxuries on my watch."

One of the fedora-wearing men reached for the solarium door, and they both strode through it as Irving's muscles twitched. He started mumbling, "Extortion, embezzlement, bribery, price fixing."

Dotty and Leon sidestepped away as fast as they could. Leon apologized for getting her involved. "I didn't know Irving was against unions. I've gone and jeopardized my chances of becoming a waiter this weekend." He raised his head and asked, "Do you think Eva has returned by now?"

She wanted to remind Leon that Eva's heart belonged to Hershel, but she kept quiet. Then again, maybe Eva would be ready for a new fella soon.

At the Colonial, Leon burst into their room first and cried out, "Are you all right?"

Eva was lying on her bed with a wet cloth covering her forehead. "I'm just resting."

Leon's expression held both concern and suspicion. Dotty opened the curtains that had been drawn closed. "You better get ready; it's wise for us to be at our stations earlier than usual. We must impress Irving to get back on his good side," she told Leon.

Eva removed the cloth and peered at them.

Leon blinked and shifted from foot to foot. "Irving caught us going to a union meeting. He's not happy about it."

Eva locked eyes with her. "Don't go messin' with unions unless you want to be on the next bus departing for the Bronx. And don't be surprised if Irving gives you the worst station tonight." Eva wagged her finger at Leon. "I thought you wanted to be a waiter."

"I want to be just like Irving one day."

Dotty watched Leon's knees knock together and reached for her Lucky Strikes.

ABE

Abe stood outside Irving's office. A whiff of cigar smoke blew from under the door.

"Unless you're the union captain, you can come in!" Irving yelled gruffly.

"I'm sorry to bother you, Boss."

Irving held a thick cigar in his right hand. "You are smarter than Leon for not having attended the union meeting. I'd suggest you talk some sense into him." He raised the cigar to his lips.

"I will, Boss." He was too nervous about his family situation to focus on any guilt.

Irving exhaled a plume of smoke. "Eva should have warned Dotty about my disdain for unions."

"Dotty was at the meeting?"

"She and Leon were planning to attend until I put my foot down. If they want to be employed under me, they had better not go to any more union meetings."

Now he could not ignore the guilt in the pit of his stomach as he stared at the large pegboard. He had heard about the unique way "King Cupid" kept track of where everyone sat. This was his first time seeing it up close.

"You like my system? The pink pegs represent the women and the blue pegs represent the men. I keep track of ages and whether they are single or married by lighter or darker shading. I pride myself on placing nice, single, Jewish girls next to nice, single, Jewish boys." Irving turned his back to the pegboard and asked, "What brings you by?"

"My papa surprised me unexpectedly, and my ma is on her way. They don't get along. I'm here to request that you seat them far apart."

"That can be arranged. I don't want any unpleasantness in my dining room if it can be prevented."

"Thank you. My ma is the more difficult one. I'd like to bus the table where she's sitting so I can keep an eye on her."

"You're doing a swell job, Abe. How'd you like to carry your own tables?"

"I'd sure fancy waiting tables, Boss."

"Keep up the good work and you'll be rewarded." Irving leaned back and puffed on his cigar.

He walked outside and perched on a stone wall. The afternoon sun was directly overhead as he prayed that Papa was still resting. Five minutes later, his sister disembarked from the hack, carrying a new brown leather suitcase. It was an improvement from the *schmata* bag she had *schlepped* from foster home to foster home as a toddler.

Ma trudged behind with a scowl on her face. Jean wrapped her arms around his waist. "Oh, Abe."

He hugged her back fiercely and directed his question at Ma over Jean's head of curly dark hair.

"What's there to frown over? You're in the beautiful countryside."

"I miss the ocean already, and my legs hurt from being cramped up."

Ma must have been eating plenty of helpings at dinner. He could not imagine how she had fit into the hack, given its tight space. She had wrapped herself in a cloak of fabric and painted her face with thick makeup. He inhaled the sweet smell of her familiar perfume and kissed her on the cheek.

"I have a headache from all the yapping."

"Come, let's put your stuff away and get you fed so you'll feel better." He picked up Ma's extra-large bag.

Ma's face softened after she stepped into the lavish lobby.

"I want to go play shuffleboard," said Jean.

"You can do all the activities tomorrow. Dinner first," he told her.

Ma slogged through the hallway. "My mattress better not be too soft."

Arthur Winarick was in earshot. "You want a more solid mattress? I'll have it delivered to your room."

It was Jean who said, "Thank you."

Ma had moved on to inspecting the drapes.

"My wife sewed those herself," Arthur said, his chest filling with pride as Ma pinched the material between her thumb and pointer finger.

Abe held his breath, praying she would not use her spiteful tongue again.

Arthur kept the mood pleasant. "We say no to

nothing around here. If you want your sheets changed twice a day, we'll have them changed twice a day for you. Are you not satisfied with the paint on the wall? We'll repaint it a color to your liking."

He did not miss the upward flicker of Ma's lips. Abe nodded at Arthur in gratitude before his stomach sank at hearing her say, "We should've gone to Grossinger's. It's only about 15 minutes away. Let's call a hack."

"I think you'll find the Concord is superior once you're settled in," said Arthur.

Abe steered Ma through the hallway, eager to put distance between her and the big boss. He had just removed the room key from the lock when Ma spewed her next complaint. "It's too dark in here."

Jean opened the curtains before placing her copy of *A Tree Grows in Brooklyn* on the nightstand. "This room is perfectly delightful."

He was not sure how Jean maintained her cheerful attitude with Ma's cruelty slung at her so often. His heart broke each time he remembered Ma begging 14-year-old Jean to move to Brighton Beach. Jean had agonized over the decision to leave the foster home where she was loved and taken care of to live with a mother who had rejected her at age two. Once Jean had reached Penn Station in New York City, Ma changed her mind and told Jean to go back to Philly. He had never wanted so badly to wring Ma's neck. He had gone to get Jean from the train station and brought her to Brighton Beach himself. Ma had to kick a boarder out so Jean could have her own room.

Jean handed him a letter from Al. He had written

that he had seen Milton Berle perform for his troop and enjoyed the show. Abe could not wait until he and his older brother could sit around swapping stories in person again.

"I have to start setting up the dining room," he told them as Ma admired a gold chain under the light of the lamp. Jean was hanging her dresses in the closet when he caught her eye.

"Ma, I'll give you privacy to change into your dinner attire," Jean said.

He held the door open and followed his sister into the hallway. "Papa's here."

Jean gasped. "Papa is in the mountains right now?"

"He sure is, and only one floor away."

"Oh, Papa," Jean exclaimed. "I must say hello. I bet Minnie is in a dreadful state. She always says traveling makes her ill."

"You'll never believe it—he's here alone!"

Jean put her hand to her chest. "Is Minnie sick?"

He shook his head. "Papa finally ditched her."

"Permanently?"

"No. I wish."

"We all wish that," Jean said as Ma threw the door open.

"Come unpack," Ma barked.

It was left unsaid that they would not tell Ma her ex-husband was at the Concord. He waved goodbye and traipsed to the Colonial, worrying about who would have to serve Ma.

Leon was shaving in front of the mirror and halted his grooming to say, "I have to warn you. Don't ever accept a thing from anyone involved with a union again. It'll upset Irving."

He had forgotten all about the union stuff and withheld his role in the trickery. "Sorry, pal." An extra lively dinner was closing in. He rushed to change into his bussing uniform.

In the dining room, Irving came right over to him. "I placed your mother at Dotty's station. She deserves the more challenging of the two. Your papa will sit at one of Eva's tables. They'll be on opposite sides of the room. I'll let you choose your station since Leon's in hot water."

He chose Dotty's station and shook Irving's hand in gratitude. She deserved a heads-up that his ma was difficult.

CHAPTER 8

Dotty had not had much contact with Abe since Eva said he had been with the dancers inside the Rio Cabana. She was not thrilled he was her busboy tonight, but she would maintain a professional demeanor.

"I want to apologize in advance for my ma's awful attitude," Abe said.

"Your ma is here? Leon said it was your papa."

"They are both here. It's a coincidence."

"How nice that they came to visit you. I can't wait for my parents to experience the Concord."

"They are divorced and can barely stand to breathe the same air."

"*Oy vey.*"

"My younger sister Jean is a real sweetheart. She'll be sitting with Ma. She always tries her best to keep Ma tame. However, it's a no-win situation. Ma will be one of those 'I'll have a taste of everything' guests."

Armed with that knowledge, she would bring lots of samples to the table. "Where is your papa going to sit?"

"I spoke with Irving, and he put him at Eva's station."

Obviously, Irving had given her Abe's mother as a punishment. She would do everything she could to get back in her boss's good graces, and how bad could Abe's mother really be?

Soon the dinner guests streamed into the dining room. Irving led a robust woman with a teenage girl to her 10-top. She guessed it was Abe's family. The woman seemed as carefree as can be, delighted by the attention. Abe must be worried for no reason.

"Hello, I'm Dotty," she said after Irving strode away.

"I'm Jean, and this is my mother, Ida."

She admired Jean's mint-green, shawl-collared dress. "Your dress is beautiful."

Jean was all smiles.

"I don't like my food burned," Ida growled. She readjusted the brooch clasped near her bosom on her satin dressing gown; it was her idea of Friday night dinner attire.

Ida's heavy rouge applied to her cheeks reminded her of a clown at the circus. "I'll let the chef know." Dotty faked a smile.

"Oh, Ma, I know all the food will be delicious," Jean said.

"Don't overfill my coffee cup either." Ida let out a snort.

Now she understood what Abe had meant. She hoped the demure husband and wife from Port Jefferson were all right. They had been prompt to every meal, and now their seats remained open at her 10-top. She was not pleased they would have to sit beside Ida.

Irving, walking rather heavily, escorted a new guest to the empty seat next to Ida. "What about the Gersons?" Dotty realized this man was the same man she had seen several times already and most recently entering the union meeting.

"I moved them over there." Irving motioned for her to step aside to have a private word. He lowered his voice and said, "Don't let him convince you to attend any more union nonsense. I'm not giving him a dime of my wages, but I will pay special attention to your table. We don't want any trouble during dinner." Without further discussion, he headed to the maître d' stand.

She bit her bottom lip, resigned to the fact that Irving was still punishing her.

The gangster flung the menu aside. "And coffee."

Fine, she would bring him a house salad, matzo ball soup, and a ribeye. After memorizing the rest of the orders, she increased her gait in the direction of the kitchen.

Sautéed tiny mushrooms seemed like the perfect treat to present to the table for everyone to share. Right away, Ida plucked one between her greedy fingers and held it in the air.

"All the food is tasty, Ma," Abe said, refilling water glasses.

Ida bit into the mushroom, took her time chewing, and spat out, "Not enough *taam*."

Dotty saw both Abe and Jean exchange looks of frustration. Then Jean smiled and said, "There's plenty of taste, Ma."

Ida turned toward the man next to her. "What's your name, and what do you do for a living?"

Dotty was glad she was not carrying a tray of food, or she would have dropped it on the floor.

The gangster licked parsley from his fingers. "You can call me D.R. I'm a businessman."

"I'd have thought you were a medical doctor with those initials. My husband's a businessman, too."

Dotty held her breath.

"Who knew from business?" Ida shrugged and asked, "Who's the headliner tonight?"

Dotty released her breath and thanked her lucky stars that Ida did not pursue asking him more about his line of business.

"Sammy Fain," a guest across the table said.

"Will he be any good?" Ida asked.

"Good ol' Hershel would never book him on a Saturday night if he weren't terrific," said D.R. before cracking his knuckles and cackling.

"He's performing a late-night show over at the Brickman Hotel after he's done here," said a guest over his bowl of chilled apricot soup.

"I heard Sophie Tucker's going to be over at the Tamarack Lodge," volunteered another guest.

"Sounds like they got the better act," Ida said. She reached over and stuck her finger into Jean's matzo ball soup.

"Sammy Fain is talented," said D.R., his chunky pinky ring clinking against the edge of his soup bowl.

"He doesn't know from…" Ida flung her wrist in the air. "I should go over to Grossinger's on Saturday night."

"I'm going over to the G later myself. There's a union meeting there tonight." D.R. winked at Dotty and slurped down his soup.

Now that she knew a darker side to labor unions existed, she wanted to curb any more discussions about it. Aiming to exude confidence like Hershel, she said, "The Concord has the best Saturday night show. There's no reason to go anywhere else."

Ida glared. "This chopped liver needs more

schmaltz."

Abe was right there to whisk it away.

Dotty ran her *tuchus* off. Careful to avoid eye contact, she placed the ribeye in front of D.R.

Ida tossed her cloth napkin aside, stood up, and announced to the entire table, "I'm using the washroom."

Thankful for the tiny reprieve from this combative woman, Dotty had immense sympathy for Abe. She watched Jean race over to Eva's 10-top as soon as Ida had thumped her way out of the dining room.

"That must be your papa," she said to Abe, who was stacking dirty bowls and keeping one eye on the door.

A guest at her 8-top was calling for her, so she hustled over. While this guest detailed, in excruciating detail, what dairy products did to their digestion, she heard shouting.

ABE

"*Shtick drek*! I lived a joyless existence, Nathan!" Ma screeched, clamping onto a pumpernickel roll.

Abe crumbled his face into his hands. The current situation was exactly what he had been afraid of happening.

"*Ligner*!" yelled Papa, shaking his hands at the ceiling. "You were always lusting after other men."

"Suspicious, suspicious, suspicious, and you never even gave me an extra *shekel*, holding the purse strings so tight." Ma's face was a deep shade of red. She swung her arm around and threw the pumpernickel roll at Papa's head.

A collective gasp was heard throughout the dining room. Jean pushed her way to the center of the action. Abe's heart broke for his younger sister. Papa's small-framed body looked tiny in contrast to a crazed and voluptuous Ma.

"How'd you buy all that jewelry, the mink stoles, and extravagant clothes, Ida? I was your husband!" Papa yelled.

"You were a peddler with a cart, saying *kaddish* for people at the cemetery. Did you think my button sewing could feed all the mouths in our family? You couldn't afford anything," Ma squawked.

"At least I didn't get one of the children killed and abandon the others to be raised by strangers."

The onlookers gasped again, even louder.

"Who killed whom?" a woman cupping a hand over her ear called out.

"You said you were at the store buying milk, but that was a lie. You left the *kinder* locked inside the summer porch, and our sweet Milt died because you were trying to woo a man into taking you to the next theater opening."

"How was I to know Milt would pick up a match and a tin of shoe polish? The explosion wasn't my fault."

Abe stood between his parents; his elbows held out to separate them. Jean wrapped her arms around Ma's torso, trying to tug her away. Irving was encouraging guests back into their seats.

"I'd like some coffee," D.R. called out.

Abe saw Dotty tear herself away from the wild

scene to retrieve a fresh pot. He charged forward, forcing Ma toward her seat. He just had to make it through dessert.

"With the way you threw the pumpernickel roll, you could pitch for the Brooklyn Dodgers," D.R. told Ma. He cackled again.

As Abe caught Jean's eye, flashing her all his sympathy, two chocolate chip cookies flew past him. Ma had hurled them at D.R., saying, "Wasn't the reign of Murder, Inc. in Sullivan County over when Jack Drucker went to prison?"

D.R. brushed crumbs from his jacket with one hand and slowly stuck his other hand in his back pocket. Ida stood smirking at him. Abe was mortified.

D.R. tossed a coin onto the white tablecloth. "You're a hawkish old lady," he told Ida. He turned to Dotty and jutted his chin at Eva. "I'd tip you better, but she stole my money."

Abe was on guard, watching D.R. saunter toward Eva's table. Irving, always aware of the happenings in his dining room, cut D.R. off, escorting him to the exit.

"She's too thin," Ma pointed at Dotty. "Give her some of my dessert. It needs more sugar, anyway."

"She doesn't want your leftovers, Ma." He swatted away the plate of apple strudel.

"Everything is delicious," Jean reported on her end.

"Try Jean's babka. It's too dry."

"Ma, I'm working. I can't eat right now."

"Do what I say Abe-*ala*."

He pivoted his head to make sure Irving was preoccupied before biting into the dessert.

After Ma ordered every type of cake on the menu and complained about every slice, she was ready to head out. "What are we going to do now that dinner is over?" she *kvetched*, lugging her handbag over her shoulder.

"Let's go listen to music," Jean suggested.

"I'm tired. I'm going to bed," Ma growled.

Chapter 9

DOTTY

Dotty's heart ached for Abe's little sister, who it appeared craved maternal affection so greatly that she put up with anything slung at her. During cleanup, she asked Abe, "Is your papa all right?"

"Papa is resilient. My parents' marriage was always stormy. They were two greenhorns in the middle of a dreadful depression. Papa traveled to the USA from Ukraine, not knowing a single person. He met Ma and fell instantly in love."

She knew her own parents' marriage was one of convenience, but there was also real love there. Her ma traveled from Russia to Ellis Island, and her papa's ship sailed from Poland to Boston.

"I should be happy the *shtarker* named D.R. didn't pummel Ma for throwing cookies at his head," Abe said, his arms full of dirty linens.

Eva overheard, "She didn't dare."

"She sure did," Dotty said.

Both she and Eva keeled over in a fit of laughter until Irving stood before them, and they straightened right up. Leon, standing to the side, shot her a warning look.

"I've assigned you and Leon to mop the floors in the kitchen tonight," Irving said.

"You never should've gone to the meeting. You're lucky you are still employed here," Eva whispered.

"That gangster says you stole his money," she whispered back.

"I need to speak with you, Eva," Arthur Winarick

said.

Dotty went to retrieve a bucket and soap.

ABE

When Ma thumped her way out of the dining room, Papa scampered over. "My *kinder*," he said, his voice softening.

"Oh, Papa. I'm so happy to see you," Jean cooed.

"Sammy Fain is playing the piano tonight," Abe reminded them.

Jean did a little jump into the air. "Oh, we must go see him."

Papa agreed.

"I'll finish in here and meet you inside the nightclub."

Jean's face brightened at getting some rare one-on-one time with Papa.

"Let's go play shuffleboard, Papa."

Abe resumed his cleanup duties and saw Eva shaking Arthur Winarick's hand. He hoped their talk had nothing to do with his union scheme. When he saw Dotty and Leon carrying mops in the far corner, the guilty knot returned to the pit of his stomach. He rushed to finish, eager to meet up with his family.

Dotty caught him before he exited and handed him a scalloped-shaped purse. "Jean left this at the table."

"Thank you," he said, looking at the dirty smudges on her white uniform.

She bowed her head in shame. "I'm filthy. Mopping is no fun."

"I owe you an egg cream for dealing with Ma tonight." His guilt was back; she had to pay to get her uniform laundered.

"I'm a fan of egg creams, but it might take a baker's dozen to compensate for your ma's lack of manners. She has quite the sharp tongue and bothered all her tablemates."

He would not defend Ma—he never did. He could not imagine Dotty's reaction if she learned how heartless Ma was, discarding motherhood for a lover who gave her the life she felt she deserved.

"The chef will spit in her soup tomorrow if I repeat what she said about his food." Dotty yawned. "I must go clean my uniform and get some sleep."

"Irving will forget all about the union stuff soon enough."

"I hope you're right. I'm headed straight for a shower." She yawned again and waved farewell.

For a moment, when he reached the Rio Cabana, he stood in the back and observed Papa and his sister. Out of all the siblings, Jean resembled their father the most. Papa had once admitted to him he had been furious after Jean was born, assuming Ma had been unfaithful because he had only ever fathered sons. Life without his lovable younger sister in it was inconceivable. He ordered a seltzer and cranberry cocktail and carried it to her, waving at Arthur and his wife in their front-row seats.

"I'm checking out tomorrow after breakfast," Papa announced.

Jean frowned.

"You aren't going to stay through the weekend anymore?" he asked.

"I think it's wise to return at a different time than

Ida's visit."

Abe understood, but still, he frowned, too, as Papa reached for both of their hands.

"I'm going to recite a *brucha* to keep Al and Norman safe."

"Can we say a prayer for Milt as well?" Jean asked.

His heart swelled on hearing his deceased older brother's name for the second time that night. Jean had never even met Milt, yet she held him in her heart always. Abe had been a 6-month-old baby during the fire that ended 2-and-a-half-year-old Milt's life. The miracle that he and Al survived unharmed was something he would never take for granted.

A gray cloud crossed Papa's face, and he bowed his head. He had been a rabbi back in Ukraine and would have loved to continue his rabbinic studies in America. It had been his goal to lead a congregation. Unfortunately, his luck never panned out.

As Papa ended his prayers, Sammy Fain sat down in front of the piano. The three of them, tapping their feet, watched in awe.

"Oh, Abe, I forgot I have another letter for you." Jean sorted through her purse after Sammy's performance and pulled out a white envelope.

He tore it open and read every line. The final sentence was of particular interest. "Five bucks says you can't lose your virginity within two weeks of being there," his pal back in Brooklyn had written.

He was always interested in a good bet, certainly with that amount of money on the table. Boy, oh, boy, would he like to add five bucks to his wallet.

"What's it say?" Jean sipped at her seltzer and cranberry juice cocktail.

He winked. "Just a little bet between friends."

"I'm so happy to be back with one of my brothers." Jean gave him a tight hug.

He squeezed her back, knowing she was also wishing Al and Norman were with them. "We'd better get you back to your room. We all know Ma wakes up with the birds."

Jean looped her right arm through his and her left arm through Papa's. They dropped Papa off first. Abe walked Jean to her floor, whispered goodbye, and kept watch until her door clicked shut.

Hidden in the shadows, inches from the Colonial's front door, he overheard two other busboys conversing. "Irving told me he'll give me a shot at carrying tables soon."

Up to that point, he had not considered the competition. If he were not the one to land the job, he would want it to be Leon, and he had sabotaged that. He undressed, wrestling with guilt over his hoodwinking, and fell into a fitful slumber. Leon was snoring next to him.

CHAPTER 10
Week 2, Friday

DOTTY

Startled awake, Dotty saw Eva stuffing cash under her mattress. It was the witching hour, so she pulled the covers to her chin and rolled over. The next time she opened her eyes, a slice of sun was poking through the curtains. Eva was still bundled under blankets, but she had questions ready. "Where were you so late?"

Eva stretched her arms above her head and kept her eyes closed. "Arthur wants to hold a charity poker game here at the Concord with the proceeds going to veterans. He asked me to help. I was practicing my poker skills in a midnight game."

She assumed Eva won since she caught her hiding money under her mattress. Glad to know that was all that Arthur had wanted to speak with Eva about in private, she got out of bed.

"There's a spot for you at the table." Eva threw back her covers and retrieved the new box of cards Dotty had bought at the sundry shop. "Start practicing, or you'll make a fool of yourself."

She hopped onto the edge of Eva's bed. "We have time for a quick game of Gin Rummy."

Eva faced the deck down and started shuffling.

***

Dotty dropped a sugar cube into her coffee. Eva put her hands on her hips and stuck out her bottom lip. "Are you still in the doghouse?"

Eva wasn't done pouting over her early morning card loss yet. Dotty said, "I hope not," and took her first sip.

"Good morning," Hershel said, appearing out of the blue and stepping forward to kiss Eva on the cheek.

Eva stepped back and wrinkled her nose. "Why are you up so early?"

"A *gonif* was trying to sneak in."

"The Concord has the tightest security around. It's impossible," Eva said.

"They always think they can be the first person to skate by the guards and make it past the front desk. No way, not on my watch." Hershel flexed his muscles.

"D.R. ate in here for the first time last night at Dotty's station."

Hershel put his hand on the small of Eva's back. "Pardon us, Dotty, we're going to take this conversation to the hallway."

She finished her coffee, her mind racing with questions. *What did the initials D.R. stand for? What was buried? And what was the message Hershel had received from prison?* She crossed her fingers that the gangster was still sleeping, worn out from a night of illegal behavior.

With droopy shoulders, Abe found her. "Irving assigned me to your tables. He's letting Betty carry an extra table in the interim."

She turned around and saw the aging waitress with ace bandages wrapped around her ankles and calves, smiling with Irving. Betty suffered from arthritis and moved slower than the other waitresses. Many business owners would have cut her loose a long time ago.

Abe was stoic. "My time will come."

So what if he had been mingling with dancers the other night? Everyone had the right to enjoy some fun. She decided to let bygones be bygones and visualized the egg cream he owed her. "I hope your ma woke up on the right side of the bed this morning."

"She never does."

Jean came to breakfast alone. She wore a fashionable blue and white polka dot dress. Dotty asked, "Where's Ida?"

"In bed with a headache."

She beamed with joy over the fortunate break.

Abe had overheard. "Ma's sick?"

Jean shook her head. "I think she's avoiding Papa. Can he move over to my table now?"

Abe zipped over to Irving with the request.

Dotty seized the moment to speak with Jean and asked her, "Are you enjoying yourself here?"

"Yes, and I don't want to ever leave."

She, too, wished she never had to leave. At home among the mountains, she knew that come Labor Day she would be a puddle of tears.

"I was a toddler when I went to live in foster care. My brothers always protected me."

"Foster care?" She forgot all about her future end-of-summer woes.

"When Ma abandoned us, Papa learned we were eligible for assistance from the Juvenile Aid Society."

She tilted her head and raised an eyebrow.

"Someone created it for Hebrew orphans. Papa was a peddler and couldn't afford to keep us with him, so we had to live with a new family."

She watched Abe hustle about. There was a lot

more to learn about him.

"At one of the homes where they placed us, they supplied only one single bed, and all four of us couldn't fit. Abe volunteered to sleep in a chair—for months."

Her heart ached over Jean's story, but she had to turn her attention to the other guests. As kids, she and her sister slept on a pull-out sofa in the living room, under the train tracks. It was a million times better than sleeping in a chair in a stranger's house. She counted her blessings.

Jean soared out of her seat to welcome her father to their table. Dotty offered him some juice and went to the kitchen to retrieve the pear nectar flavor he requested. The tray in her hand wobbled upon her return when she saw Ida in the dining room.

"Why is this *shtick drek* in my seat?" Ida squawked. Her peach-colored dressing gown dipped into a V, revealing her curvy bust to the crowd.

Abe came to her rescue and steadied the tray but jabbed his elbow too far to the right just as a guest was about to eat a spoonful of her breakfast. Somehow, the woman ended up face-first in the bowl of cottage cheese; her wig got caught in the whole ordeal.

"He tore my wig off. He should buy me a new one!" yelled the woman, no more than 5 feet tall, shaking her blonde bob-cut wig at Abe. The woman's natural hair was a soft shade of silver.

"You'll get it in my oatmeal!" screamed another guest.

Dotty covered her mouth and looked at the ground. She hoped a comedian was watching and crafting a joke.

Irving charged over. "We'll take you to the on-site beauty parlor right after breakfast, Mrs. Klein."

"You have cottage cheese on your nose," Ida barked at Mrs. Klein as Irving, holding the wig, guided the woman back to her table.

"We'll get you a new wig before your birthday lunch," Irving said. He bared his teeth at Ida.

"*Oy vey.*" She considered hiding in the kitchen instead of turning back to her stations. She saw Nathan's trembling hand clutching his juice glass. Ida started wrapping napkins around "for later" danishes and stuffed them into her handbag.

Abe gestured to Nathan's previous table. "Ma, we moved you over there."

"We're leaving. *Fartick*," Ma barked.

"But Ma, I haven't finished my griddle cakes, and you said we were staying through the weekend," Jean pouted.

"*Ligner!* What else is new?" Nathan mumbled.

Dotty prayed Ida had not heard what her ex-husband had said, but she went ahead and braced for an explosion. Sure enough, Ida whacked Nathan across the back of the head with her handbag.

"Ma, let's go right now." Abe tugged her across the dining room as a forlorn Jean gave Nathan a bear hug. Ida hollered from the doorway for Jean to hurry.

Waving goodbye to Jean, Dotty knelt by Nathan and asked him, "Are you all right?"

He touched his palm to his forehead. "I'm tougher than I look."

Abe returned to the table. "Now I really owe you an egg cream. How about today after our lunch shift?"

Butterflies flapped their wings in her chest. "Since you show none of the same traits as your ma, I'll agree to it."

She finished her duties and stopped by the sundry shop to buy Q-tips. Her eyes landed on the front cover of the latest *Republican Watchman*.

Local Boy Jack Drucker:
The Last of Murder, Inc. Sent to
Attica Prison

"You want to know about his crimes?" Marv asked.

"Yes."

Marv leaned forward on his stool. The top button of his navy vest, his daily uniform, popped undone. "I have a cabin in Rochester. My Uncle Joe, who worked for the Erie Canal, left it to me in his will. It's not too far from Attica. I don't make it up that way much with my business here to run. And I certainly will not visit Drucker during my vacation there." He rubbed his eyes.

She looked down at the picture of the ice pick and shuddered as the shopkeeper buttoned up his vest.

Marv put his elbows on the counter. "This here is an informative article. It starts by telling about the time a carpenter noticed a trail of blood that ended at Drucker's barn. The police search uncovered human remains, but the crime wasn't pinned on Drucker. It wasn't until Walter Sage was found floating on the surface of Swan Lake, with a fatal ice pick wound, that Drucker was wanted for murder. Sage was a hitman who helped himself to profits off slot machines. Stealing from Murder, Inc. was very dangerous. They stabbed him 32 times and tied his body to a slot machine before dumping him in the lake."

The gruesome tale caused her to cover her mouth with her hand.

"Federal Agents pursuing Drucker discovered bodies in Monticello, Loch Sheldrake, Liberty—all over Sullivan County. It wasn't easy for them to catch ol' Jack hiding out in Delaware. The key to the prosecution was Albert 'Tik Tok' Tannenbaum, the son of a hotelier from Loch Sheldrake. He turned state's evidence against his former boss. After the biggest trial ever seen in Monticello, a jury reached a guilty verdict."

She grabbed the Q-tips; her head was spinning with information overload.

"Here, take a matchbook," the shopkeeper said, tossing it into the bag on top of the Q-tips. "I got a bunch in today. I think the design is quite nice, don't you?"

She glanced down at the tiny picture of a full moon shining over mountains. Then she chose a piece of peppermint candy to calm her nerves. She would not let gangsters and prisons dampen the mood.

ABE

The woman with a wig was a grandmother of 14. She was celebrating a milestone birthday with her grandkids. Irving sent out a chocolate sheet cake with chocolate icing and instructed his staff, "Go sing to her with enthusiasm. She's been staying here since Winarick acquired the Concord as a primitive boarding house."

Her new, upgraded wig was blonde and curved toward her ears with a rounded back and curly layers.

Abe belted out the tune and tried to stay in the background in case she was holding a grudge. The sing-along elevated the mood. The rest of lunch qualified as a good meal.

While washing silverware together, Leon said, "I hear they need waiters over at the Nevele."

Eva handed him a spoon that had fallen to the floor and overheard, "I'm not ready to hang my hat up at the Concord yet."

As she walked away, Leon whispered, "I think I'll stay here, too."

"You can't be sweet on Eva. She's with Hershel."

"Hershel is a womanizer," Leon said, his expression serious.

Abe carried the clean silverware back to his station and dumped it out onto the tablecloth to dry. Dotty helped with the task. "Shall we get that egg cream?" he asked after they were finished.

"I need to change out of my uniform first."

"I'll see you at the coffee shop in 30 minutes." He had some time to kill, so he decided to try his hand at swinging a golf club.

"Leon, do you want to hit some golf balls?"

"I've never golfed. I'd like to learn."

They saw Arthur Winarick tuning his viola in the lobby. Leon stopped. Abe had heard that he was quite the viola player, but his mind was on golf.

"I'd fancy hearing him play a song," Leon said as Abe nudged him along.

On the practice green, he held his putter in his hand and practiced keeping his head down. He saw two of the dancers he had met inside the Rio Cabana. His eyes went directly to the hemline of their dresses.

"Why don't you come and enjoy a nice beverage with me?" Fran, the dancer, asked.

She struck a pose on the manicured grass, and he gripped the putter.

"What about Dotty?" Leon poked him with his golf club.

It was true; he had plans, but now this gorgeous dancer was standing right in front of him. He wrapped his hand around the warm hand of the dancer, paying no heed to his conflicting emotions.

The other dancer tried to grab Leon's hand. In a flustered voice, he spat out, "Uhh…I forgot I must speak to Eva about the charity poker game."

The dancer whose hand Abe held giggled, and the other dancer rubbed against the closest caddy. He briefly doubted this was the best course of action, but the five bucks popped into his mind, and his manly instincts took over.

CHAPTER 11

DOTTY

"Are you sure I can't get you anything, hon?" the coffee shop waitress asked, glancing at the clock and then at the napkin Dotty had torn to shreds.

As Dotty crossed her legs, the smell of grilled cheese filled the joint. She jiggled her foot inside the vinyl booth and swept the pieces of the napkin into her hands. Then she shook her head and listened to the conversation in the booth behind her.

"Why is it called an egg cream if there are no eggs or cream in it?" a child sipping one asked.

"To make it sound fancier. I've heard people think saying 'egg and cream' sounds expensive," the adult with him said.

She agreed with the good explanation as she watched the waitress carry a plate of French fries with brown gravy to the booth across the room. A little sugar from the flavored syrup in an egg cream would take the edge off her worry. She signaled to the waitress.

"Here you go, hon." The waitress slid a foamy, filled-to-the-brim egg cream in front of her.

She held the long-handled spoon and dipped it into the milk, carbonated water, and syrup. Ma would scold her for consuming so many calories between meals. Finally, with no Abe in sight, she sighed into her empty glass and gave up.

"Did you enjoy yourself?" Eva asked, raising her eyes from a notepad when she returned.

"Abe never showed up."

"You don't say? Come, sit." Eva patted her mattress. "I've been studying ways to ensure I win the charity poker game."

"What do you mean?"

"Have you ever seen a marked card?"

She gasped. "That's cheating." Ma had told her about a woman she played with in the Bronx who was always trying to mark her cards.

"I'll just mark the aces."

She scooted to her side of the room. "It's a charity game. We should stick to the rules and be honest."

Eva's fiery eyes glared at her while she swatted her hand through the air. "I'll donate to the veterans. Oh, come on, live a little."

Perched on the edge of her bed, she was afraid of doing anything to cause her to get stuck on permanent mop duty. It did not sit well with her to cheat in this situation.

"I didn't peg you for such a goody-goody," Eva scoffed.

She walked straight out the door without responding. As the warm sunshine cascaded down around her shoulders, her Lucky Strike eased her neck and shoulder tension. *Ma always said that winning fair and square made you feel larger than life.*

"Hello, Leon," she called out.

"Hello, Dotty." He slowed his fast pace.

"Do you know if Abe is all right?"

Leon kept his eyes on the horizon behind her. He was acting in a strange manner before perking up. "I've come to see if Eva can help me prepare for the charity game. I need to learn some tricks."

She flicked her cigarette butt onto the ground. "Eva's in search of a co-conspirator."

Leon twisted his face into a curious expression and ducked inside the Colonial.

ABE

As Abe prepared for dinner, he saw a kitchen worker squawking and jabbing his finger in the air, imitating one of the chefs. "You get nothing. Only the fish guts."

The second Shabbat dinner was off to a bang, and the guests had yet to appear. He was chuckling at the spot-on impersonation when Leon jabbed a finger into his back. "You ditched Dotty for the dancer. You said you were a gentleman."

His gut tightened. He tried to embody a gentlemanly demeanor consistently, but at times, his intentions fell short. "Did Eva share all her poker secrets with you? You don't want to step on Hershel's toes, do you?"

Leon hunched his shoulders. "I don't want to end up as fish food."

"You'd be wise to find yourself a different sweetheart."

"Eva deserves a man who is devoted exclusively to her." Leon crossed his arms.

"Do you want Hershel to pummel you?"

Leon stuck his nose in the air and turned on his heel as Dotty approached Abe from behind and tapped his shoulder. "I hope everything is all right."

"I apologize. Something came up. I've worked it out now," he said, flitting his eyes to the ground.

"I'm glad to hear that."

Betty, the waitress with ace bandages, was carrying on. "They are unfriendly. I refuse to serve that table anymore."

"I'll switch with her," Dotty volunteered.

That caused the tantrum to end. Irving said, "Very good."

Eva brushed past Dotty. "I guess you don't want to mop floors again."

Abe fiddled with his glasses, not pleased with the tension between the roommates.

Dinner fell solidly in the "good" category. At the tail end of the cleanup, Dotty told him, "I'm exhausted. The table I gained in the switch was friendlier than I anticipated. They all had appetites equal to elephants, though."

"You aren't kidding. The matriarch ordered three helpings of the grilled chicken livers and cleared every plate."

Dotty yawned. And yawned again. "I'd still like that egg cream." Her cheeks flushed.

He tapped her nose. "I think you need your beauty sleep right now. I'll see you at breakfast." He watched her exit. He was wide awake and went moseying out of the dining room. His feet were on autopilot as he headed in the direction of the Rio Cabana.

Hershel greeted him with a glass of scotch. "Do you want to make some money over at the Grossinger's basketball game on Monday night? The chef at the G promised a couple of players that he'll cook them the best steaks they ever tasted. They just have to throw the game by six points."

"That sounds like a pretty good deal."

"So, you see, we bet against the G with insider information that we'll win. The guests are completely in the dark about the fact that scores are fixed in advance. They don't know the players are throwing games for the bets."

"Sounds like quite the racket." Abe was okay playing a little dirty. "Bring me to the next game, why don't you?"

"It's real nice knowing your gamble is going to pay off." Hershel clinked glasses with him.

"That's my favorite kind of gambling. I fancy setting my eyes on Grossinger's."

Fran shimmied through the entrance of the nightclub. He smoothed down his hair as she click-clacked over.

"It's Friday, the one night they don't have to perform. They are supposed to rest for the Sabbath." Hershel winked and handed him another drink.

He finished his scotch on the rocks in a couple of swallows and eased into a corner with the dancer. As they necked, the door slammed open.

"I'm here for the money," D.R. growled. "Time is ticking."

D.R. was a lot more menacing outside of the well-populated dining room. Fran's fingernails dug into his thigh. Boychik slunk from the corner, showing his teeth.

He had an arm around Fran's quivering body. *What the hell was happening?* He kept his eyes glued to D.R., whose left hand was concealed in his pocket. After a few more words with Hershel, out of Abe's hearing range, he prowled away. Fran waited a moment before yanking him out of the door with her.

The hours slipped by and night turned into dawn as he realized that he needed to untangle himself from the dancer's embrace. Because he was victorious in winning the five-dollar bet, swaggering to the hotel, he held his chin high.

After his first experience under the sheets, he enjoyed a long shower, whistling and shampooing his hair. His grin was as bright as the single lightbulb hanging from the ceiling when he bumped smack dab into Dotty.

CHAPTER 12
Week 2, Saturday

DOTTY

It was early, yet Dotty was up and out, giddy for the day ahead. Plus, she was giving Eva her space since Eva was still acting pissy. Someone farther down the hallway was whistling.

"Good morning, Dot," said Abe. He avoided eye contact, only wearing pants and a white undershirt. He had his wet hair combed straight back.

Her stomach sank with distrust. Why was Abe showering when he was expected in the dining room soon? "I need caffeine." She let the door slam behind her.

A sign about a Henny Youngman show caught her attention. It lifted her soured mood. She was looking forward to watching Henny play the fiddle and tell jokes no matter what else was going on.

Coffee was her first stop. Eva burst into the dining room, a leaf falling from her hair. She must have taken a jaunt off the beaten path this morning.

Dotty collided with a busboy who was carrying a full load of silverware. She watched in regret as it all crashed to the floor around him. She apologized and spotted Abe guzzling a cup of coffee in the corner.

A busboy who qualified as a "political"—someone given the job because he knew someone—flew through the dining room with a tablecloth tied around his neck.

"What in the world? Does he think he's Superman? Did he have too many swigs from a bottle of something?" Dotty asked.

"Since he's related to Irving, they'll never fire him," Betty, the ace bandage-wearing waitress, said. She was hiccupping from laughing so hard.

Irving was shouting, "Stop the nonsense, Stanley."

Dotty giggled until Irving said, "Abe, you're assigned to Dotty and Eva today."

Despite her will to breeze through breakfast, the odds were against her. The matriarch who ordered three grilled chicken liver entrées last night wanted the same amount of challah French toast for breakfast.

She took a closer look at the busboy she had bumped into earlier, now bringing her a handful of forks after she was short a few. Maybe she would like to get to know him better.

ABE

Leon smacked Abe's arm and narrowed his eyes. "Where were you last night?"

"I wasn't a minute late for breakfast, was I?" He whistled a little tune, straightening the tablecloth on a 10-top.

"I don't think you should be messin' with Dotty's heart like that. Standing her up for an egg cream was shameful."

He did not want to think about hurting Dotty's feelings right now. He was a king on top of his mountain. "Don't ruin my good mood, pal. I finally know what it feels like to be a man, and I'd like to savor this feeling a little longer."

Leon gave him the evil eye.

Abe, his back to the main entrance, jumped in

surprise when someone smacked his *tuchus*. He came face-to-face with Fran. She leaned in and planted a kiss on his lips. He stepped back and spun around, not missing that Dotty was glaring at him.

"I'm working now," he told the dancer, wiping red lipstick off his lips with the back of his hand. "I'll meet you at Henny Youngman's show later."

She batted her eyelashes before click-clacking out of the dining room. He kept his head down and plowed forward. His emotions were all mixed up. The second he was able, he fled out the door to write to his pal in Brooklyn, informing him that he could mail the five bucks pronto—he had earned it.

DOTTY

After Abe's goofiness and the dancer's appearance, she needed fresh air. She untied her apron and chose a bench near the swimming pool. A busty woman in a stylish red and white polka dot bathing suit was flailing her arms in the water, calling for the lifeguard to save her.

Dotty rolled her eyes and watched the tan lifeguard dive into the pool. She rolled her eyes again as the woman emerged with her arms wrapped around the lifeguard's neck. A blood-curdling scream jerked her attention toward the shallow end of the pool.

"He has a knife!" screamed a guest.

Her heart skipped a beat. A guest did indeed have a knife pressed against another guest's neck. The man with the knife fumed, "You weaseled your way into my sister's room last night. I'll chop your head off."

Guests glued themselves to the scene as if it were the premiere of a long-awaited show. The knife-wielding man was not holding back, and the man in the headlock was as pale as a ghost.

They summoned Irving because he was on the civil defense. Leon must have heard, too, because he barreled over with his hands in fists. Eva was two feet behind. Irving leaped into the middle of the action. A group of female guests was in hysterics, huddled together. She wished Hershel and his muscles were there to protect them. Irving shook his fists in the air. Leon's checkered newsboy cap got knocked off his head. She did not think it was a good idea for Eva to run to his side. The knife was so close.

Irving lunged at the weapon and seized the handle. She held her breath. The threatened guest took off like a lightning bolt into the safety of the hotel lobby.

"Arthur will ban you from the Concord for life," Irving shouted at the culprit.

"I'll go to Grossinger's," the culprit shouted back.

She released her breath. Seeing Eva and Leon, with their arms around each other, did not help her heartbeat return to normal.

Chapter 13

ABE

Abe was on his way to the sundry shop to buy another postcard for Jean when an ashen-faced guest shot through the lobby. He heard the front clerk saying there had been trouble at the pool. Hershel and a bellhop jogged by, so he followed them.

They ended up at his original destination, the sundry shop. The owner stood behind the counter, his mouth agape. He stared at empty shelves and pointed to a frail woman hugging an overflowing bag to her chest. A can of tuna was sticking out of the pocket of her colonial-style dress.

"She swiped all the merchandise?" Abe asked mystified.

"And she refuses to pay me a penny." Marv had his hands on top of his balding head.

Hershel was trying to pry away the bag that the woman was clutching with both hands. The size was so large that truckloads of "for later" rolls could fit into it. He knew that normally, Hershel would've yanked the bag away, but it was a delicate situation; the woman was a century old.

"We'll have to get Winarick or call the police," Hershel told Marv, who was now pacing.

"There's never any need to call the cops," said a gruff voice.

The postcard rack obstructed Abe's view, but he could see Hershel's nostrils flaring. He stepped to the side and saw the chunky brass pinky ring.

D.R. took control of the bag and placed the stolen loot on the counter. "You're losing your marbles,

Mother." He counted out the money and slapped it on the counter next. "I told Mother not to leave the room without me. She has to stay with me while my sister is out of town." D.R. pocketed a matchbook from the pile by the cash register and steered his mother to the hallway.

"He overcompensated me. I apologize for the upheaval," Marv said after he counted the bills in a rush.

"I'm happy to come to your rescue anytime." Hershel flexed his arm muscles.

"Likewise," said Marv.

A pair of sisters walked into the shop and batted their eyelashes. D.R. barreled back into the shop. "I told Mother not to feed the stray pussycats around here." He dropped a can of tuna on the counter.

The shopkeeper was preoccupied with helping the sisters pick out a souvenir. D.R. cracked his knuckles. In a threatening tone, he said to Hershel, "Hand over the money tonight. Or you'll find your farm destroyed one morning soon. You have received a warning."

Abe ran his eyes over the shelves; he did not see any tuna fish. He figured the older woman was a kleptomaniac, also stealing from the kitchen.

Hershel, nostrils flaring again, said, "Come, Abey, we need to go to my farm right away."

Always up for an adventure, he glanced at his shoes and wished he had on his mud-stomping boots instead.

A green Ford pickup truck with a loose exhaust pipe rattled along winding country roads to reach the hamlet of Hurleyville. Hershel was behind the wheel and pointed at a white clapboard farmhouse. "That's Jack Drucker's farm. His grandparents used to run the place as a summer boarding house. Our families have been neighbors for decades."

"Murder, Inc.'s Jack Drucker?" he asked, clutching the weathered brown seat beneath him. He now worried about gangsters on top of the clunking sound coming from the truck. They passed by cows, sheep, and even a donkey.

"That's right." Hershel pulled onto a dirt path. "I suggest you don't go on his property unless you want an ice pick stuck in your back."

He vowed to never do that as he watched a goat eat grass on a hillside. He did not want anything to do with an ice pick.

Hershel parked beside apple trees. "Those are my two oldest brothers." He waved at a man leading a horse through acres of greenery and another man herding sheep. A third brother drove past in a maroon Cadillac.

Abe petted a long-haired border collie that wandered over. "It's beautiful property."

"My parents built a real nice farmstead. Let's go gather some shovels from the shed." Hershel started trekking across the recently mowed grass.

He shooed a hen out of his path while Hershel pushed the shed door open and reached for a tall shovel. Hershel then surveyed the area around the chicken coop and knelt, searching for a marker he was unable to find. "I know it was right here."

He wanted to help, but without more information from Hershel, he was at a loss. He started counting fresh chicken eggs in the coop. An old memory popped into his mind.

He and his siblings were at their first foster home. He had just woken up when the ruckus began.

"It's the most horrible thing I've ever seen—it's gross and gooey!" Jean had screamed.

Al had made a show of taking a bite of a hard-boiled egg and telling Jean, "It's delicious."

"No way," Jean had cried louder.

"I will not allow a toddler to control the situation. These are fresh farm eggs!" their foster mom had yelled.

Abe started tearing pieces from a challah loaf and tossed them onto the egg to make it tastier. Jean would not touch any of it. He, on the other hand, had eaten two eggs.

Their foster dad had come into the kitchen. He stuffed food into Jean's mouth as his wife pinned down her flailing arms. Al had knocked Abe out of the way to get to a hysterical Jean. Norman had tugged at her leg to free her from her seat. Their foster mom had thrown her hands into the air and dug into her purse for a pack of Camels. Their foster dad had cracked open a large, clear bottle of something. The next day, the Juvenile Aid Society moved them to a different foster home.

The border collie pawed at his leg. "I hope you don't have fleas," he told the dog.

Hershel stuck his tall shovel into the dirt and dug at a pace Abe worried he could not match.

"This is unbelievable. Where the hell could it have gone?" Hershel moved to another spot, muttering, sweat dripping down his forehead.

"What? Gone where?"

"The money."

Not having a clue about what exactly Hershel was hunting for, he said, "Maybe your brothers moved it."

"They don't know I buried it here. They would be outraged if they did. No one but me had anything to do with Jack."

His knees weakened. What had Hershel gotten him into?

"When I was a youngster, Jack would give me coins in exchange for collecting eggs on his property. He always treated me well. I was naïve to the fact that he was a member of Murder, Inc. until I grew older." Hershel was kicking at the dirt now.

Nothing Hershel said explained why they were searching for buried money. A brother with a strong resemblance to Hershel rode a horse over to them. "My wife left you bowls of cholent in the kitchen."

Hershel was inspecting the ground. He asked his brother, "Did you do any digging over here recently?"

"We've been busy with the crops; not much time for anything else."

Hershel threw his tall shovel aside. "Come on, Abey, let's eat."

At the wide oak farmhouse table, he moaned in pleasure as he sank his teeth into a fatty piece of brisket. "Let me guess, your sister-in-law added ginger?"

Hershel's fingers wrapped around his spoon. "How'd you know?"

"My bubbe taught me the trick: add one pinch of ginger."

"Your bubbe was right."

"Cholent was my favorite meal as a child. I'd lick the bowl clean while Bubbe shared memories of learning to cook the Jewish stew back in the old country." The farm was sparking all sorts of nostalgia.

Hershel wiped his cloth napkin across his brow. "When Jack Drucker was wanted for Walter Sage's death, the feds started hunting him. He approached me to bury the profits from his slot machine line of business. So I did. It was a tremendous amount of money, Abey. I knew I should have stayed far away from it, but telling Jack no didn't seem like the best option."

Hershel picked an already bruised red apple out of a woven basket. "Jack told me I was not to give a penny to anyone. The deal was I would receive significant compensation for the favor. Now D.R. claims he is owed half for 'bootleg bounty' and is trying to steal every penny. I did my best to send word to Jack but had no luck there. The prison even returned my call only to tell me I didn't have permission to speak with him."

Abe was scraping his spoon against his dish, not wanting to let any of the delectable cholent go to waste. "Do you think D.R. found the money and dug it up?"

"How would he know the exact spot on the 92 acres my family owns?" Hershel squeezed the apple in his hand.

"Hiding a fortune sounds like Jack Drucker took a page out of Dutch Schultz's playbook."

Schultz was a notorious gangster who buried his millions to keep it from authorities. Schultz died in 1935 and rumors were that his fortune was hidden somewhere in Phoenicia, 40 miles north of Monticello.

He dropped his spoon and stood up. *Murder, Inc. killed Dutch Schultz.* "I have to be back at the Concord soon. Saturday night dinner will be busy."

"I lost a small fortune. We'll have to resume the hunt after dinner." Imitating Babe Ruth, using his left hand, Hershel threw the apple against the wall.

CHAPTER 14

DOTTY

As Dotty went through the motions of cleanup after dinner on Saturday, she kept her distance from Abe and did her best to think about other things. Next week, an introductory Mah Jongg class was starting in the afternoon. Eager to learn the fundamentals of the game, she wiped down her station and decided she would sign up.

With loose coins in her pockets, she changed out of her uniform and headed to the sundry shop. Guests were all a-chatter, fluttering around the lobbies before the show. She observed the liveliness, and then she admired the gold pendants in the jewelry display.

Inside the sundry shop, Marv watched her select a tube of Victory Red lipstick. "That's our most popular shade," he said.

"I'll take it." She paid and used a handheld mirror to apply a layer to her lips.

"Fancy meeting you here again," said the tan-skinned lifeguard.

Her cheeks blushed.

"I was about to peek my head inside the nightclub at Henny Youngman's *schtick*. Would you care to join me?"

Elated at the idea of arriving on his arm rather than alone, she tilted her head coyly, and off they went.

Hershel, clutching his notebook, brushed by and waved. "He's a hotshot," the lifeguard whispered in her ear.

She rolled her eyes.

Eva was carrying an orange blossom cocktail, and Leon was trailing behind her. In the VIP area, Arthur Winarick and his wife huddled together, waiting for the show to begin. Hershel was now standing to their right.

Eva slid to her side and dropped her voice. "Leon's helping me mark cards." She stuck her tongue out at the lifeguard. "Don't miss breakfast."

Eva must have had more than one orange blossom cocktail by now, but still, Dotty was optimistic they had turned a corner for the better. The lights dimmed, and the lifeguard knocked his shoulder into hers. She became mesmerized by the singer and swayed to the music.

Excitement buzzed through the Rio Cabana as Henny Youngman stood center stage playing the violin. He spat out a flurry of jokes in rapid succession. His trademark line, "Take my wife, please," sent the crowd into wild hoots.

"He sure is 'King of the One-Liners,'" the lifeguard said.

She was in stitches as Henny bowed before the crowd. He waved his fiddle in the air. "Oh, what fun!" She could not wait to tell her family about it. Once the stage went completely dark, she allowed the lifeguard to tug her out the door.

"Come, I'll show you a good time."

She stared into his sparkling eyes and had an inkling she would not be returning to her room anytime soon.

Eva and Leon hurried off; she suspected they were going to study card marking.

"How about that swim?"

Her stomach did a flip-flop. "Now?"

"The temperature is warm enough. The storm isn't expected to start until early morning."

She reached for the lifeguard's hand, failing to remember that she did not have her swimsuit with her.

ABE

After Henny Youngman's show, Fran, the dancer Abe had rendezvoused with, tapped his shoulder from behind. "There you are, Abey."

Hershel set his spiral-bound notebook aside, snapped his fingers at the door, and said, "How about a swim?"

He stepped out of the dancer's embrace and leaned into Hershel's left ear. "What about the money hunt?"

"Let's have some fun." The New Jersey dancer jumped onto Hershel's back for a piggyback ride, and they all paraded to the outdoor pool.

He forgot to worry about anything as the pool came into sight. He made a dramatic splash into the water, only wearing his jockey shorts. Fran stripped down to her lacy unmentionables and swam over to him. The night sky, speckled with twinkling stars, created a welcome cover for their wild antics.

Doggy paddling in the shallow end, a noise caught Abe's attention. *Was D.R. back? Did he intend to drown them all in the pool?* His glasses were on a chaise lounge, so he could not see far.

The fella shouted, "Nobody is supposed to be out here at this time of night. I'm the lifeguard. I'm off duty now. If you drown, it's at your own risk."

Abe swam toward the ladder. Hershel beat him to it. With recognition written on his face, the lifeguard spoke in a timid voice. "I apologize for intruding."

It struck him as funny since the pool was the lifeguard's domain. He laughed.

The voice beside the lifeguard gasped. "Abe, is that you?"

The scantily clad dancer pawed at his ankles, trying to pull him back into the pool. He took the coward's way out and dove straight into the deep end, staying underwater as long as possible. Resurfacing, he heard Hershel tell the lifeguard, "The pool's all yours. We're going back to the Rio Cabana."

Abe rushed past Dotty. He had a ball of shame in his stomach over her finding him here involved in such nonsense. A glass of scotch would help take the edge off.

DOTTY

The lifeguard whispered into Dotty's ear. "That was Hershel, the talent booker!"

Well aware of who it was, her mood turned gloomy. She slumped onto a chaise lounge and listened to the call of an owl while the lifeguard removed his shirt. Unable to resist, her eyes traveled the length of his chiseled body.

He wrapped a towel around his torso and shook his left foot. "My hammertoe is the reason I'm lifeguarding instead of going off to war," he explained.

The memory of the scene they had stumbled

into—the unmentionables and the sleek dancer bodies—filled her mind. She rose from her chair, her breath shallow due to a lump that had formed in her chest. "I'm going back to my room."

The lifeguard held his hands out to her. Before giving him time to convince her otherwise, she avoided gazing at his bare chest and said, "Thank you for the fun evening."

She trudged back to the Colonial and gave herself a hard time for letting Abe throw her for such a loop. There she was, having a late-night excursion with an eligible fella, and she had thrown away the chance. Besides that, she was annoyed with Hershel for frolicking with that dancer.

She changed into a plain white nightgown and crawled into bed. There was an unopened box of cards resting on Eva's pillow. "Oh, Eva, you must be playing poker somewhere." She yawned and closed her eyes.

Around 3 a.m., she snapped her eyes open to loud, piercing sirens. She catapulted outside along with the rest of the disoriented staff. It was mayhem. She searched for Eva in the crowd.

Guests, discombobulated from the interruption to their sleep, clutched at each other. She pushed past them, rushing toward the fire truck spraying water on the nightclub. She put her hand to her mouth as she watched the blaze in horror.

Arthur Winarick zipped by in a frenzy. "Has anyone seen Hershel?" he screamed.

"The entire thing is going to burn down. Save the hotel proper!" Irving Cohen yelled to the fire chief.

Leon, wearing pants held up by a drawstring and no shirt, was waving his arms in the air. "Where is Abe?" he yelled to anyone listening.

Her heart dropped to her feet. The last time she had seen Abe and Hershel, they had been heading straight to the building engulfed in flames. She focused on the big, red fire truck positioned at the entrance of the main building.

Leon wailed, "Where's Eva?"

"She never returned to our room."

Leon slouched over, hands on his bent knees, and started coughing. Firemen were clearing guests from the scene.

The fire chief yelled, "The entire Rio Cabana foundation is about to collapse!"

"Boychik!" Leon straightened up and screamed. He was bracing himself to run into the flames.

She had forgotten about the cat that lived inside the nightclub. The intense heat on her face caused her to topple onto the ground. Gulping for air, her nightgown hem almost in the flames, she, too, worried about Boychik. A bellhop offered her a hand and helped scoot her to a safer location. *Ouch.* Her *tuchus* landed on something hard. She picked up a coin caked in mud.

Irving tackled Leon, but Leon refused to take no for an answer. He and Irving rolled around until Irving put him in a chokehold.

A prehistoric-looking woman, with singed white hair, was being boarded into an ambulance. The fire had scorched her long-sleeved, high-neck nightgown. *Oh, how awful that a guest got hurt.* Dotty covered her ears with her hands. All the shouting was too much as she watched the Rio Cabana cave in. She prayed she would soon wake from this nightmare.

Chapter 15
Week 2, Sunday

ABE

D.R. parked in the shadows and used binoculars to observe the fire. A chambermaid walked by, caught sight of the two of them, and doubled her pace. The small black revolver resting on D.R.'s lap was why Abe had obeyed and got into the car. Headlights from a maroon Cadillac had shone through the darkness and disappeared around a bend at the same time D.R. had pointed a gun at him. It was also when he lost track of Hershel.

Once the ambulance siren was too low in the distance to hear anymore, D.R. revved the engine. The Pontiac Streamliner sped toward the bottom of the mountain away from the fire at the Concord.

The breeze blowing through the open car window whipped the hair on top of Abe's head in all directions. He watched the fast, patchy indigo storm clouds, willing rain to spit down and save the Rio Cabana. The Pontiac accelerated around a corner. He leaned into the door, his heart thumping. "Where are you taking me, and where is Hershel?"

D.R. gripped the steering wheel with white knuckles and increased the speed. "Until someone starts telling me where my money is, one by one you are going to start to disappear. I wanted Hershel—you're just collateral damage."

Roads with hotel billboards turned into a secluded, dense landscape. The winding route led to Hurleyville. Abe held his breath as they passed by Jack

Drucker's white clapboard farmhouse. He was relieved they were not pulling into Drucker's old driveway, but his heartbeat continued to pound. D.R. hurtled down a dirt path and came to a stop only a few yards away from the chicken coop.

In one solid movement, Abe lunged out of the passenger door. The word disappear was echoing in his mind.

"Take the shovel out of the trunk and start digging." D.R. pointed the revolver at him. "I have a place I need to be that I did not anticipate. I'll return in a couple of hours and you better locate my money by then."

With no choice but to obey, he stuck his shovel into the ground. After the Pontiac powered forward into the night, he threw the shovel aside and turned on the flashlight he had secretly taken from the trunk.

Since he already looked for the money in this same spot with Hershel and found nothing, he started to hurry toward the dark farmhouse. Farmers had early morning chores—that made him hopeful that one of Hershel's brothers would soon help.

The long-haired border collie came from behind and licked his ankle as a voice yelled, "Abey!"

He shone the flashlight right at her face. "Eva! What are you doing here?"

She squeezed her eyes shut until he moved the flashlight to the left. "D.R. stranded me here and told me to keep digging until he returned."

"You too?"

"Where's Hershel?" Eva rubbed dirt from her arm.

The first clap of thunder roared in the distance. "I wish I knew. After the fire started, D.R. forced me into his car alone."

Eva swiped her wrist across her forehead; a dirty smudge remained. He sensed she was holding back a lot of pertinent information. He scratched the dog's head and kept what he was thinking to himself. *Hershel may have sped away in a maroon Cadillac.*

"What fire?" Eva yelled.

"The Rio Cabana went up in flames."

Eva's face drained of all color. "How awful!"

The border collie growled, and Abe stood at attention. Eva stepped nearer to him. He directed the flashlight toward the car coming down the dirt path.

The dog barked. Eva whispered, "Should we run?"

His heartbeat was strong and persistent. He wished he still held the shovel. The first drop of rain hit his forehead, and the dog barked again. Someone switched on the front porch spotlight on the farmhouse.

A broad-shouldered, heavyset man got out of the car that had just skidded to a stop at the end of the dirt path. "I'm here to return you to the Concord. Get in," he said.

Eva threw herself right into the car. Abe's face was pale, and his legs were shaky as he followed suit.

"I'm Sy." A jazz station filled the black Buick sedan. Nobody was chatty. The rain pelted down.

He realized they were not going in the right direction, and his stomach sank. He held the flashlight; it was his only weapon. Eva must have realized at the same time because her body started shaking.

In Rock Hill, the car pulled into a dark parking lot. "Welcome to the Dodge Inn, where gangsters dodge in and dodge out all night long," Sy said. The tone of his voice was light and friendly.

He studied the simple décor of the establishment in front of him while Eva asked, "Why are we here?"

"Sorry about the delay getting you back to the Concord. I can't miss the high-stakes poker game. I'll drive you back right after I win the jackpot. I promise." Sy winked.

Not sure whom to trust, he watched Eva perk up over the word poker. He chased her inside the restaurant. The rain was at a lull. "Let's hope I make it out alive," he mumbled and ran his eyes from the top to the bottom of the smoky interior. The luscious, meaty smell of steak, potatoes, and stewed onions perked him up.

A man holding a deck of cards ran straight at Sy. "The nightclub at the Concord burned to the ground."

Sy ripped the deck of cards out of the man's hand. "How can that be? Any idea what caused the fire?" he yelled to anyone listening.

If Abe had to guess, he would say D.R. must have had a hand in it, but for now, he stood there speechless.

"None at all," answered a man from the corner.

A round of thunder began as the image of the Rio Cabana ablaze was strong in his mind. He did not think he could play any sort of game at the moment. A nice-sized stack of cash beside a pile of chips changed his mind, and he pulled his wallet from his pocket in a hurry.

Lightning flashed, followed by more thunder as

he dropped into an empty wooden chair.

Sy sat at the head of the table and shook the deck of cards in the air. "In case you're mistaken that I'm a member of Murder, Inc., I can assure you I'm not. Never was and never will be. I just happen to be a well-connected, informed man with lots of sources. I'm also involved in a lot of investing. I was at the farm, surveilling Eva, about to rescue her when Abe got dropped off there as well. I'm surprised I didn't hear anything about a fire ahead of time. As soon as this game is done, I'll start looking for answers." He divided the cards into two piles and shuffled them. The rain picked up again.

The lights flickered and the room went pitch black. A man slunk out of the shadows carrying two tapered candles. Abe worried he was a gangster. Sy seemed unmoved, tossing another wad of cash onto the table and dealing the deck.

He picked up his hand. Eva grimaced, staring at her cards. He focused on the two aces he held instead of the condition of the Rio Cabana or Hershel's whereabouts. The roof rattled.

DOTTY

Irving was saying something, but Dotty's ears still rang from the loud sirens. Her hands curled around a blazing cup of black coffee. She concentrated on his lips.

"Leon will be your busboy for breakfast," he said, his forehead wrinkled.

In all the pandemonium, she had forgotten it was Sunday; she would be collecting tips soon. Abe was going to miss out if he did not resurface soon. The pool incident hours before the fire had her emotions about him conflicted. She touched a strand of her damp hair. It hadn't occurred to her to grab an umbrella for the short journey from the Colonial to the main hotel.

"Any word from your roommate?" Irving asked.

"None at all." She bit her bottom lip.

Irving announced, "We have canceled the charity poker game until further notice." He hurried to the dining room captain.

It was the right decision to postpone it, with the fire and Hershel's disappearance. At least now Eva would not be able to cheat. A twitch of concern for the dancers from the pool the night before nagged at her. Were they unaccounted for as well?

The name Jack Drucker repeated over and over in her mind. Should she tell her boss that Eva and Hershel got tangled up in some funny business with him? Could his associate, D.R., who was prowling around, have something to do with the fire?

Leon, his eyes sunken and scared, tapped her on the shoulder. His frown was so deep it seemed to hit his shoes. "I have had no luck finding Boychik."

"He's probably just playing hide-and-seek." She tried to sound convincing.

They moped through setup. Leon bent over to tie his shoe when she saw him leap up and exclaim, "Abe, Eva, you're back!"

She whipped her head around. She, too, saw their friends run into the dining room at the very last possible second.

ABE

"Abe!" Leon said, wasting not a second to hug him tight.

"You can't get rid of me that easily."

"Don't make light of the situation. You and Eva could have ice picks stuck in your backs by now."

He stepped out of Leon's embrace and counted his lucky stars. First, Sy had saved him and Eva at the farm. Then, after Sy won the jackpot at the Dodge Inn, he kept his word and drove them back in time to be at breakfast.

"Where's Hershel?" Leon asked.

He raised and lowered his shoulders. A flashback of the fleeting glimpse of the maroon Cadillac near the fire clouded his mind—and a memory from visiting Hershel's farm the first time surfaced. One of his brothers had been driving a maroon Cadillac. *What was going on?*

"Any news on how the fire ignited?"

He shook his head back and forth. He had not slept a wink and needed coffee immediately. He thought of his brothers, who would accuse him of lying after he wrote to them about playing poker at a gangster's hangout. And he did not want to scare Jean, so he would not say anything to her at all.

"I'm glad to see you're okay," Irving said, sneaking up behind him as he guzzled his hot cup of joe. "You'll bus Betty's tables today."

He set his coffee cup aside and hustled over to Betty's station. He forced a smile for the benefit of the first guest, who had her hand to her heart. Every guest wanted to know every single detail of the fire.

"Well, who started it? Will they go to jail?" asked one guest.

"I heard Kid Twist's ghost might be back," said another.

"Kid Twist is the canary that could sing but couldn't fly. He tumbled out a window in Coney Island while under police custody. You're dreaming if you think he's alive in the mountains," spat another guest before biting into a piece of honeydew.

"Perhaps it was an electrical fire?" Abe said.

The distressed guests were about to become unruly. Luckily, Irving had a tight hold on the reins, and the staff followed his lead.

Dazed by the events that had occurred, he managed to get through breakfast and then lunch. He drank a lot of coffee and then collected tips. His pockets were very full.

After lunch, he saw a couple of bellhops moving tables into the busy lobby for a handful of guests who were hesitant to drive home in the rain. The decks of cards beside the Scrabble board made him think of Sy. If not for Sy, he was not sure what fate would have bestowed upon him the previous night.

Surveying the land where the Rio Cabana used to stand tall, he saw a heap of rubble. *Boy, we are lucky there were no casualties.* He headed back to the Colonial when Fran burst out of the shadows.

"There you are, Abey. Everybody was concerned. Where's Hershy?"

He stepped back. "Wish I could tell you."

The dancer giggled and placed her hand on his arm. "Don't you want to spend some time together?"

She batted her eyes.

Exhaustion settled into his bones. He filled his lungs with the temperate air and said, "I better get some rest before dinner."

She continued to bat her eyes. A sudden thirst to cool things off with her had him adding, "I have responsibilities."

The dancer puckered her lips and stuck her chest out. Dotty happened to walk by. He shifted his eyes to the dancer, who was not budging, then back to Dotty, who had halted in her tracks.

The dancer twirled a lock of hair around her finger as Dotty decamped in the opposite direction. He escaped to his room and locked the door.

Chapter 16
Week 2, Monday

DOTTY

The lights remained off as Dotty slipped into her yellow uniform and stumbled onto the edge of her bed. She winced, and Eva began to stir. "Didn't mean to wake you," she whispered.

Eva threw back her covers and sat up. She reached for the opal-shaped heart, which was no longer at her throat, and her face crumbled. "I can't believe the deranged gangster ripped off my necklace and tossed it out the car window like it was a spoiled piece of gefilte fish."

"We'll get you a new one."

"It was one of a kind," Eva wailed. "This is a bad sign of things to come."

Spooked by superstitious talk, she heard staff rushing to breakfast and became anxious to be at her station. She was reaching for the doorknob when a swift knock and a bright-eyed and bushy-tailed Leon opened the door.

"What's the story, morning glory?" he asked.

Eva perked up. "There's a basketball game over at Grossinger's tonight. I happen to know the outcome is already settled." She winked. "The G will throw the game by a half-dozen points."

"Don't you think you should be searching for Hershel instead of attending a game?" Dotty asked.

Eva stuck out her lower lip. "I don't know where to begin."

"How about with D.R. and Jack Drucker?" She

had no advice on how to do that, though.

Dotty edged Leon out the door while Eva stayed behind to get dressed. A heavy-footed Irving met them upon their arrival in the dining room. "Have you heard anything from Hershel?"

She wished she could answer "yes" instead of "no."

Abe entered the dining room, and the night at the pool flashed into her mind. His grin irritated her. She finished setting up and welcomed her new guests, who had many questions.

"Where will we go to see shows from now on?"

Irving, within earshot, swiftly answered, "Arthur Winarick is building a new, state-of-the-art nightclub. It will seat over a thousand guests. He's naming it the Cordillion Room, and it will have an adjacent bar called the Night Owl."

She pictured a luxurious showroom.

"Is Danny Kaye still performing here on Saturday? How will the show go on without the talent booker?" asked another guest who had been eating lox.

"You bet he is. The show will go on no matter what. We'll turn the dining room into a nightclub if we have to," Irving said.

Arthur Winarick, with several sheets of paper in hand, found Irving. "I've already put feelers out all over Sullivan County. I'm going to hang these on trees in Monticello."

She was able to read the blocky handwriting announcing a reward for Hershel's safe return. It was only Monday—he had plenty of time to return for the big show.

"I'll put one right in front of Kaplan's on Broadway. The new delicatessen is attracting large crowds. Maybe somebody will know something," Arthur said.

"What did the police chief have to say?" Irving asked.

"I'll check in with him later. He only left the scene of the fire about a half hour ago after sifting through the rubble for hours. It was his suggestion I hang signs. He gave me his word that he will do his best to dodge the pesky newspaper reporters."

"I promise the chief will get the best cut of ribeye during his next meal here," Irving said.

She understood the code; the biggest hotel owners liked to keep bad news out of the papers. They had special relationships with the police to accommodate that.

"I'll call Einhorn and Troper," Arthur said. The two men booked talent at most small venues. "Maybe they can shed some light on the mystery of Hershel's fate."

Irving hushed his voice so much that she had to scoot closer to hear him ask, "Did a gangster put a hit on the nightclub?"

The throbbing vein in Arthur's neck caused her to hightail it to the kitchen. She was holding a fresh pot of coffee when she crossed paths with the dancer who she had seen with Abe the night before. Jutting her hip to the right, she nudged a busboy into the fragile little thing's path. She covered her mouth, faking dismay at peaches and scrambled eggs ending up in her wispy, strawberry-blonde hair.

ABE

Crash! Breakfast dishes rained down around Betty, the waitress who had wrapped an additional ace bandage around each of her lower limbs. Carrying the extra table must have aggravated her bones and joints even more.

Abe rushed to the scene and bent down to pick up the broken pieces. "Take over for her. Leon will help bus your tables," Irving said.

He jumped into waiter mode.

"Apple griddle cakes and rye toast," Leon translated for the 8-top table of mostly Polish-speaking guests.

He was thankful for his pal's help. He skedaddled off to the kitchen where the kitchen steward was in a huddle with the dining room captain. He seized the opportunity to stack 16 mains with aluminum lids onto his tray.

The kitchen steward crossed his arms and blocked his path. "You know the rules: no more than 12 dishes allowed."

"If I don't serve both of my tables at the same time, they'll complain." The steward stayed until he removed four dishes, his eagle eyes monitoring every move.

A station away from his own, he saw Irving hand Fran a towel. *Why did she have food in her hair?* The loaded-down tray was so heavy he needed to stay in motion.

"Abey," he heard Fran say. He grew flustered and set a plate of cantaloupe and a plate of apple griddle cakes in front of a male guest.

"What a piss-poor waiter," the guest mumbled. "I

asked for puffed rice and a fluffy onion omelet, and I got this."

"Oh, dear. I'll be right back with the correct order," he scolded himself for the error. Here he was, his first opportunity as a waiter, and making a fool of himself. At least it gave him a reason to rush away from Fran. He touched the bow tie around his neck. It was still in place as he hustled.

Back at his station, he found Arthur at the table. "How is everyone this morning?" Arthur asked.

The guest who had received the wrong food raised his fork in the air. "Don't expect me to tip him if he can't even get my breakfast order correct."

His stomach turned as he stood in front of the big boss, embarrassed by his mistake.

"I have the best staff. I don't hire any second-rate people." Arthur loped off.

Had Arthur, who believed the guests were always right, even if they were wrong, defended him instead of reprimanding him? There was time for this to turn into a good meal.

"Look what was in my wife's food!" screamed a guest.

He leaned in and saw the toothpick that must have fallen inside a bowl of oatmeal by mistake. "Are you sure she didn't drop it in there?"

The guest scoffed.

He stood back and said, "*Mazel tov*, you've won a free bottle of wine. We were playing a game. Whoever found the toothpick is the winner!"

"My wife could have injured herself if she swallowed it."

Irving arrived on the scene and glared at him. He turned to the guests and put a hand on each of their shoulders.

"I'll be right back." Abe sprinted to the activity director and explained the situation.

The activity director grabbed a bottle of Manischewitz for the Bergs from White Plains. "I'm here to announce that you're our winner! Let's give them a round of applause."

He clapped his hands together, avoiding Irving's eye. The Polish-speaking guests called for him. He searched for Leon and almost knocked over a tray held in the air. He apologized, "Sorry, Dot. Didn't see you there."

She narrowed her eyes and said, "Just like you didn't see the toothpick." She dropped her voice lower, "And just like I didn't see the dancer beside me."

He narrowed his own eyes. She zipped off and he listened to the cacophony of sounds. Hopping to it, he called out to the Bergs who were in transit to the exit, "I hope you enjoy your Manischewitz."

The husband clutched the bottle in his hands, and with a shy expression, asked, "Might we get Danny Kaye's autograph after the show on Saturday night?"

"I'll see what I can do." He winked at the Bergs and swallowed hard. How would he make such a request come true without Hershel's help?

The Bergs' smiles traveled from ear to ear.

A guest wrapped an entire tray of danishes with napkins and dumped them into her handbag. "Fa later," she said, catching him watching her.

"Don't mess up my lunch," said the guest, still

upset about the wrong food he had received.

Abe gave the man his friendliest wave, confident he would never mess up his order again. He loosened his bow tie and breezed through cleanup, his adrenaline pumping.

At lunchtime, he did get every single order correct, and then he went to relax outside. The birds were singing as he sniffed at the air that smelled like a Cuban cigar. A hand reached out and touched his shoulder.

"Hershel?" he yelled, spinning around.

CHAPTER 17

DOTTY

After lunch, Dotty stood scanning the rubble. She thought she would find Eva here. A tree branch snapped behind her. *Achoo.* She sneezed and rummaged around in her purse for a tissue. *Achoo. Achoo.* A cat must be near.

Boychik leaped from the shadows, spitting a large hairpin at her feet. He was a little worse for wear. His striped tail was missing a patch of fur, but he seemed energetic and healthy otherwise.

Achoo. She picked up the item he brought her. She turned the hairpin around in her hand and slipped it into her apron.

She expected to find Eva back in their room, yet it was empty. She wrote to her parents and underlined the sentence telling them she wanted to stay in the mountains after the season ended. She folded the letter and realized she was short an envelope. She walked over to Eva's side, knowing exactly where she kept her stationery pack.

Under the bed, her fingers first touched a copy of *The Heart Is a Lonely Hunter* by Carson McCullers. Then she grabbed hold of a legal pad with notes on card marking and threw it aside. She found an envelope. As she stood, a spiral-bound notebook caught her eye. She stretched her arm out and pulled it closer. "It's Hershel's notebook!" she shouted into the empty room. She looked at the door, confirming that she had locked it, and whispered, "What if the notebook contains a clue?" She rushed to flip through the pages. Hershel had listed the date of the show at the Concord and the performers' names in neat rows. Danny Kaye's name had a star above it, and Hershel had scribbled, "Can't miss DK's show," beside it. She flipped past George Burns and Gracie Allen's entry and kept flipping until she found the pages that listed the big hotels in alphabetical order on one side of the notebook. The schedule of performers and their appearances was on the other side. Impressed by Hershel's organization, she read over several entries. But her unease was too strong. With no clues, she closed the notebook and put it back where she found it.

Her mind raced with malicious thoughts. She stuffed the letter she had written into the envelope and wrote her parents' address on it. The notebook was priceless to Hershel. It did not make sense why Eva would keep it hidden. What did Eva know that she wasn't letting on?

Eva came barreling into their room. "Slip into comfortable shoes, Dotty, so that you can come with me."

She fidgeted with the envelope in her hand. "Where are we going?" Her gaze went toward where Hershel's notebook was hidden.

"To town to eat at Gager's Diner. It'll be nice. We'll let a waitress wait on us for once." Eva pulled a taupe silk scarf from her dresser drawer and handed a Prussian blue one to Dotty.

Her unease had not gone away, but going to town was an adventure she did not want to pass up. "As long as I'm back for the next meal." She grabbed the hairpin and tucked it into her handbag.

"Follow me." Eva pushed back her shoulders.

The sun-drenched mid-afternoon made her envious of all the guests at the pool. She squinted into the warm rays as Eva stopped in front of a red convertible and dangled a key in the air.

"Whose is this?" she asked, scanning the car from top to bottom.

Eva wrapped the silk taupe scarf around her chestnut-colored curls and did a little curtsy. "It's mine. Get in."

Speechless, she pulled thick, plastic-rimmed sunglasses from her handbag. *Eva must be involved in bigger gambling stakes to afford such a car.* Still, she sat her *tuchus* in the luxurious passenger seat. She rolled the Prussian blue scarf into a triangle before securing it on her head and tying it under her chin. Her uncertainty faded as the car rounded the corner. Fresh mountain air encircled them. She decided to focus on fun. Worry could wait until later.

Eva came to a stop in front of the rectangular Gager's Diner, smack dab in the middle of Monticello. Dotty stuck one leg out of the car onto the tree-lined street, pretending to be a Hollywood star. She removed the blue scarf and ran her fingers through her hair as two pedestrians strolled by arm in arm. A stocky police officer at a quick pace, in pursuit of two teenagers, crossed the street further up. She raced up the two steps into the diner, surveying the booths pressed against the windows, and followed Eva to a corner one.

"We'll have a pastrami on rye with two Dr. Brown's Cel-Ray sodas," Eva told the waitress. The waitress wore a white uniform with a red name tag and fire-engine red lipstick that matched her nail polish.

Dotty nodded that she liked the idea of splitting a sandwich. Eva fiddled with her cigarette case and kept both eyes glued to the window beside her.

She could not contain herself any longer. "Where did you get such a car?"

Eva blinked several times. "I found some money."

The waitress set two Cel-Ray sodas, with straws sticking out, onto the table. Unsatisfied with Eva's vague explanation, she sipped her soda. An image of Hershel horsing around with the dancer at the pool the other night popped into her mind. She had not mentioned it to Eva, and now it did not seem like the ideal time. She unzipped her handbag and threw the hairpin onto the table.

"Huh?" Eva was eyeing the large silver hairpin.

"Could be evidence. You won't believe who dropped it at my feet."

"Who?"

"Boychik!"

"He survived the fire?"

"He sure did. We have to figure out who this hairpin belongs to." She knew tons of them existed. How in the world would they be able to determine who dropped it? She had seen the same exact ones for sale inside the sundry shop. She tucked the hairpin back into her handbag as the door jingled open, and the waitress brought over a pastrami sandwich as tall as the Empire State Building. She bit into it and almost choked on what she heard next.

"D.R. is here." Eva curled her hand around a fork.

Her appetite disappeared. She worried that D.R.

might have a machete under his jacket. And a pistol. A tap on her shoulder caused her to rise a foot out of her seat.

The gangster's sneer revealed a crooked grin. "Hello, cookie. It's my favorite waitress at the Concord."

Her heart rate quadrupled. She saw a Monticello Hospital sticker on his jacket.

D.R. tore the sticker off. "My mother suffered an accident." He slapped the sticker onto the tabletop, his chunky pink ring clanking into Eva's glass. "Hand over my money. Or, people might end up in worse shape than the patients I just saw at Monticello Hospital."

She turned to Eva for answers. Fainting was a real possibility.

Eva held eye contact with D.R. "Release Hershel."

"Couldn't even if I wanted to because I don't know where that scoundrel is hiding. Where's my money?"

Eva maintained a poker face and guzzled the Cel-Ray soda.

"I bet you know exactly where Hershel is right now. You are likely assisting him in hiding!" D.R. bent down and put his palms on the table. "Where did you get the car you are driving?"

Eva sat without showing any emotion. A lightbulb went off in Dotty's head. She was pretty sure she knew how Eva had purchased the Ford Deluxe.

D.R. was tapping his watch. "Time is ticking."

"Release Hershel," Eva said again.

D.R. slapped the table with his right hand. "Let

me inform you of what my nickname stands for." He licked his lips.

Dotty gripped a fork.

He cackled. "Drucker's Rat. That's right. As in Jack Drucker." He cackled more.

"Murder, Inc. ended, and Drucker is in prison," Eva said.

"He'll be appealing real soon. Return the money," D.R. growled. "Time is ticking." He strode to a booth on the opposite side of the diner.

She slithered out of her seat. "Let's leave," she hissed, focusing on the copious dessert display near the doorway.

"I should've spilled hot coffee on him," Eva hissed back before waving over the waitress.

They paid in a hurry.

"Look," Eva pointed to a sign pinned to a tree trunk.

"That's Arthur's work. I saw it this morning."

Eva stepped closer to the sign. "I could use that reward to help pay back Drucker's *gelt*."

"So, you HAVE been messin' with dirty money."

"You are the only one who knows." Eva placed her pointer finger over her lips and made a "shhhh" sound.

She gawked at her until a man in a dapper brown suit, with a satchel, stepped onto the curb and went to the sign. He scribbled on a notepad with a sharp pencil.

Eva was tying the taupe silk scarf around her curls and asked, "Who are you?"

"I'm a reporter with the *Republican Watchman*,

the best weekly newspaper around. This story will make the front page. Between the fire and the missing talent booker at one of the largest hotels," the reporter trailed off, blowing air out of his cheeks. He shook his notepad and pencil in the air.

"I suggest you go inside right away, and you just might land the scoop." Eva winked and snapped her fingers at Gager's entrance.

She swallowed hard. The *Republican Watchman* came out on Friday mornings. Surely, by the end of the week, someone would solve Hershel's disappearance, and it would no longer be newsworthy.

Taking a leaping stride into the diner, the reporter said, "I do crave a cup of coffee."

"Should we warn Arthur?" she whispered to Eva.

"Not yet."

"Did you pay for this car with the money D.R. was talking about?" She claimed the passenger seat.

Without missing a beat, Eva wiggled into the driver's seat and then put her foot on the gas pedal. "Yes, and I know where the money is concealed. Not even Hershel knows that I moved it next to the haystacks by the pond on his family's farm."

"When did you do this?"

"Thursday night."

Stunned, she swatted at a mosquito that buzzed through the open window. She pictured Eva sneaking around on a dark, shadowy farm. "Weren't you playing poker after meeting with Arthur?"

"It was a perfect cover story, wasn't it?"

She could not disagree with that. Dotty held onto her handbag as Eva turned with urgency. "You must return this car. It has to have cost a fortune. Hershel needs to come home."

"I'm sure the dancer from the pool will be happy to welcome him back."

She took a quick breath. "You know about that?"

"I'm no fool. Why do you think I'm waiting to hand over the money? Hershel deserves to squirm for a couple of days—wherever he is. I don't know where that is! And I deserve to have some fun with this car before I have to resell it."

She kept her eyes on the terrain ahead as she processed everything she was learning.

"Before the fire, I even took Hershel's notebook to punish him for his debauchery. I never expected him to disappear, honest to God!"

She let out a deep breath, relieved that was the reason Hershel's notebook was under Eva's bed.

ABE

If only the bellhop he had seen earlier smoking the Cuban cigar had been Hershel, he would have been more confident in his answer to the Bergs. "I think we'll be able to get you that autograph."

Of course, Abe did not mention the toothpick incident. He set a bowl of beet horseradish on the table for all the guests to enjoy during dinner. He aimed to please and earn the best tips he could.

"Our son won't believe it," said Mr. Berg.

He forced a pleasant expression. With no solid plan for getting Danny Kaye to sign a menu, he held his head high and believed it would work out.

The Polish guests needed his immediate attention. *Crash!* A monkey dish smashed into pieces on the floor. "We need a broom." He snapped his fingers at Leon, who was serving as his busboy. He couldn't let the Monday night meal turn into a bomb.

Abe glided through the dining room, holding his left arm high above his head. He bounced around, accommodating everyone until dessert plates were licked clean and guests threw back their chairs. He paused to catch his breath and loosen his bow tie. Tomorrow, he would send Jean a postcard telling her he had successfully carried tables all on his own.

"You survived," Irving said.

He puffed out his chest, a proud look on his face. "Thanks for the opportunity, Boss." He saw Leon clearing the livestock. "I'd better help him."

"I'll give you a chance through the week. We'll see how things are going by the weekend," Irving said before brushing past him.

His boss's words gave him the extra jolt he needed. He scanned his eyes over his empty station. He wasn't going to skimp on anything during his first night as a waiter. Ready to go, he heard his name and saw Eva waiting for him.

"To think you were my busboy your first night in the mountains and you're already a waiter. You're making moves, Abey." She held a lit Lucky Strike between her fingers. "Perk up, we're going over to Grossinger's. There's a basketball game."

His memory flashed back to Hershel, who had clued him in on the game. His gut tightened over the disappearance of his slippery pal. Without him here, he did not have the energy or enthusiasm to attend. He rolled his head around his neck, eager to jump into a hot shower.

Eva did not budge. "Have yourself a Coca-Cola. You and Leon are going to the G with me. I have our ride all taken care of."

He saw she meant business and knew it was best to go along with her plans. He would rinse cold water on his cheeks and save the shower for later.

DOTTY

Dotty reached for the pills on the midlevel shelf.

"We can't have one of Irving's finest waitresses ill," said Marv, moving the stool he had been resting on behind the counter.

"These will help prevent a monster headache." She shook the pill bottle in the air and noticed the shopkeeper was only wearing a white dress shirt today. *Where was his vest?*

A new issue of a car publication resting on the counter grabbed her attention. She pointed to a car that resembled the same one she had ridden in with Eva earlier. "How much does it cost?"

Marv fought a yawn. "Quite a pretty penny."

She presumed as much and handed over a coin.

"Wish I could afford such a car. My caddy has a ton of miles on it." Marv covered his mouth while he yawned.

"I hope you get some rest."

"I will tonight. I haven't slept much since the arson," he said.

His eyes were dimmer than usual, and the way he said "arson" with conviction made her shudder. She followed his line of vision to the basket of matchbooks beside his cash register. *Where was Hershel?* She waved farewell as Marv yawned once more.

In the lobby, she saw Arthur Winarick. He was with the head of maintenance, reviewing the plans for the new nightclub.

She had to step out of the way because a bellhop was flying through the hallway. "Boss!" he screamed.

The loud voice made her temples pulse more, yet her curiosity was too strong to leave without hearing a possible message about Hershel. She massaged her scalp with her fingertips.

"There's been a response about the reward sign, Boss!"

She unscrewed the top of the aspirin container and popped two into her mouth.

CHAPTER 18

ABE

"Is Dotty with you?" Leon asked.

"She has a headache. We'll bring her a cold soda pop on our return," Eva said. "Come, I'll drive." She wrapped a taupe silk scarf around her curls.

Abe doubted the headache was real; it probably was an excuse to avoid him. Agitation over Hershel's disappearance remained in the pit of his stomach. Even so, he was pumped for the basketball game and strutted outside.

As they walked by the area where the fire had destroyed the Rio Cabana, Leon fretted. "We need to search for Boychik."

"Don't worry, Dotty saw him earlier. He survived the fire. That stinkin' cat has eight more lives to live," Eva said.

Leon perked up when Eva unlocked a fancy red convertible. He hopped right into the passenger seat.

"Hot diggity dog—this is no jalopy," Abe said. She must've won one hell of a poker game to be able to drive around in a Ford Deluxe. He sat in the back and gazed at the streaks of orange and pink in the evening sky with his arm resting out the side. He could not believe it was Eva in control of the steering wheel. A loose lock of chestnut-colored hair was sticking out from the silky scarf tied around her head. He could tell why two of his pals were keen on her affection, but he did not like being caught in the middle.

"We have one stop to make first. I want to see if Sy has uncovered any insider information on Hershel," Eva said as their stylish ride cruised through rural roads to the Dodge Inn. Eva came to a stop and removed the scarf she wore while driving. Leon observed her with puppy dog eyes.

He rolled his eyes at the two of them and trotted inside. Sy was sipping a rye whiskey at a round table. A deck of cards was on his lap.

"What about the basketball game?" Leon raised his voice and asked.

Eva swept her hand through the air. "They have already decided that outcome. Let's play some poker."

Sy finished his rye whiskey. "It's another high-stakes game, sweetheart."

She placed a neat stack of cash on the table beside the chips. "I've been winning a lot." She batted her eyelashes.

Abe let out a low whistle and whispered in Leon's ear. "She must be winning a *whole* lot with the car she was driving." He waited to hear if she would mention the original reason why they came to the Dodge Inn, but her mind was only on poker now.

Eva shook her pointer finger at Sy. "You better not mark any cards."

Her comment set Sy off into a fit of laughter. "I have a new deck right here." He ripped the plastic off the package with his meaty fingers.

Leon pulled him aside and whispered, "Do you think it's a good idea to play poker with gangsters?"

"Sy isn't a gangster," he whispered back. "I'll take my chances. It might come in handy to keep a guy like him around, especially since Hershel isn't here."

Leon turned his nose up at him. Abe looked toward the kitchen, wondering how many steaks were sizzling on the grill before rejoining the poker table.

Sy threw back the rest of his whiskey. "You think you can beat me? All right, well let's see about that."

Eva grinned with a self-satisfied expression as Sy shuffled the new deck. Two more fellas threw money onto the table.

Someone passed around a silver flask. Abe took a gulp and passed it to Leon, who took his turn imbibing before Eva tipped her head back and let the liquor slide down her throat. The empty flask signaled that it was game time.

On Abe's turn, he chose to fold. Leon hung in for another hour.

It was Eva who ended up vaulting from her seat. Everyone's jaw dropped at the sight of a rare straight flush. She curtsied and held her hand out.

Leon's tense posture showed he was ready to fight for the winnings if he had to. Someone threw a wad of cash onto the table, and Eva snatched it right up.

"Nobody wants to play again?" Sy raised an eyebrow.

Abe was considering one more game as he cleaned his glasses with a cloth napkin.

"I have five dollars to start the next game, but you must tell me what caused the fire and where Hershel is right now." Eva clutched her purse filled with money.

"Unfortunately, I still don't have answers for you—yet—but I'm giving it my best shot to get to the bottom of it."

"Are you a detective?" Leon stepped out of the shadows.

Sy shuffled the cards. "Used to be. Handed in my

badge after I was told I turned a blind eye when it came to ethics."

"Well, do you?" Leon asked.

Sy laughed. "If I feel it's warranted, I don't like letting bad guys get away." He divided the cards into two stacks.

Leon tapped Abe on the shoulder and pointed to the exit, but Eva did not budge. Two hours later, to Abe's shock, he threw down a full house and jumped out of his seat with a triumphant grin. As he scooped up the significant amount of money, Eva harrumphed and knocked her chair onto the table.

"Let's go," she said with an edge to her voice.

Back inside the Ford Deluxe, he closed his eyes, and the cool breeze whipped against his face. At the gates of the Concord, he climbed out of the car first. When he looked over his shoulder, Leon was leaning in and kissing Eva smack dab on the lips. He walked to the Colonial alone, worrying there would be real trouble after Hershel returned.

Chapter 19
Week 2, Tuesday

DOTTY

"I'm glad to see your migraine is gone," Eva said, clad in her yellow uniform already. She was rubbing Pond's face cream into her cheeks.

Dotty spritzed a hint of Chantilly perfume onto her neck. "A full night's sleep did wonders."

"Last night was very exciting." Eva beamed at the stack of money sitting on her nightstand and hummed an upbeat tune.

The humming struck a nerve. "Why aren't you handing over the money immediately?" she snapped, annoyed by the lack of concern for Hershel.

"We don't even know if D.R. is telling the truth. Is half the money really his for his so-called 'bootleg bounty'? Does he have Hershel or not?" Eva went back to humming.

She stepped into the hallway and let the door slam shut. She instinctively knew Eva's greed stemmed from leaving Europe, but it annoyed her. She saw Abe and Leon ahead and maintained her distance. Still, she was able to overhear their conversation.

"I'd sure like my turn serving tables. How'd you get so lucky to beat me to it?" Leon asked.

"I'm as surprised as you are. It'll be your turn any day," Abe said.

Inside the hotel, she dropped a sugar cube into her coffee and searched the room for signs of Arthur. She had been unable to learn the content of the message sent to him. She prepared her stations for the breakfast crowd and kept an eye out for Arthur right up until the first guests arrived.

"What a shame," said a guest. "We came to the mountains expecting to see Danny Kaye."

Her goal was to respond the same way she imagined Hershel would. "You will still see him perform. It's going to be quite the show. The Concord has the best entertainment in the mountains. You're guaranteed to have a terrific time."

"Where will he tell his jokes now that the nightclub is a pile of ashes?" another guest asked.

"We might as well go over to the Brickman Hotel to see the show," the first guest said.

"I heard Berman and Pransky are taking over the bookings here at the Concord," said a broad-shouldered, heavyset man. He pulled out the last empty chair at her 10-top.

"You don't say," said another guest, peering down her nose.

Dotty caught sight of Abe twirling a woman wearing a felt beret and was taken aback that he allowed her to kiss him on the cheek. He was really working for his tips. She scowled in his direction.

Irving placed a bloody mary, garnished with a celery stick and a slice of lemon, down in front of the heavyset man. "Enjoy your beverage, Sy."

"Thank you," said Sy.

She tugged at her apron strings, curious why they seemed so well acquainted. Irving took notice of a young couple bickering and strode off to restore harmony between one of his newest love connections.

Sy drank half of his tomato juice and vodka in big

slurps. She took orders and hustled off to the kitchen.

Eva caught up to her as she pushed through the kitchen door. "What's Sy doing eating breakfast here? I'd have bet money he would still be asleep."

"Who exactly is Sy?"

"He's a citizen detective and he's one hell of a gambler."

She raised her eyebrows. "Can he help you find Hershel?"

Before Eva could answer, a busboy skidded into her. The bowl of Rice Krispies she was carrying crashed to the floor. In a split second, a very smitten Leon was there cleaning up the mess. Dotty wiped off cold cereal and milk that had splashed onto her arm. Duty called, and they all flew in different directions.

Afraid that Sy was linked to Jack Drucker's money-hunting associate, she placed his poached egg on toast in front of him with great care. A mix of emotions shot through her. She was waiting for a guest to ask him what he did for a living and, no more than two minutes later, she was in luck.

"I do a lot of investing," Sy pointed to the left. "Who knew Eva would be so indifferent about her fella's absence?" He bit into his egg.

She followed his gaze to where Eva was posing between identical twin male guests. The *Concord Evening News* camera's flashbulb went off. She stumbled sideways and bumped into a busboy carrying a bowl of strawberries. She sulked over the state of her stained yellow uniform.

"Come pose with us," shouted a guest. She held her tray in front of her strawberry-stained uniform and forced a smile.

Right after the bulb flashed, a guest held out their cup. "I need a refill."

"More for me, too," said another guest.

A busboy collided with Dotty. She missed her mark, and coffee spilled onto the white tablecloth. A guest with a high-pitched voice started shouting. She fought the urge to hiss "hush" and waved over her busboy. He tripped, and the grapefruit juice he had been carrying landed on her shoes. All she could do was throw her hands into the air—it was just one of those mornings. Breakfast was a bomb.

"For you, sweetheart," Sy said at the end of the meal.

She snatched the dollar bills out of his meaty fingers. "This is too much."

"Don't spend it all in one place." He winked while she marveled at the amount.

She slipped the money into the pocket of her apron, causing a button from her pocket to roll onto the floor.

"I'll be back sometime soon. It's a pleasure to be eating inside Irving Cohen's dining room. We know each other from the civil defense." Sy bent over to pick up the button.

She dropped her voice to a whisper, following her instincts. "I mistook it for a coin, but when I cleaned it last night, I saw it was a button. It has been nagging at me that I've seen that same button somewhere before. I want to compare it to the buttons on the drapes."

Sy scratched his chin.

Still whispering, she told him, "It's probably

nothing, but I found it near the nightclub when it burned down.”

Sy held the gold button toward the light. “Mind if I borrow this?” He reached into his wallet and then handed her another dollar bill.

She nodded her head, “yes.” If he kept tipping like that, she would be happy to serve him all his meals. “I hope you have a wonderful day.”

“I’m taking a drive further upstate. I have some business to take care of.” He tucked the button into his pocket and bid adieu.

Arthur stormed by, shouting, “I’m no fool!”

“That was some nerve,” said Irving.

“They thought they could steal from me and get away with it. No way am I handing the reward money over to a dishonest *putz*.”

“Tsk tsk,” she said, disappointed that the message had been a hoax.

Arthur wagged his finger right in Eva’s face. “Tell Hershel if he’s not back by tomorrow morning, he won’t have a job.”

“I don’t know where he is, boss,” Eva pouted.

Dotty was halfway to the Colonial when D.R. covered her mouth.

Chapter 20

ABE

Assigned to two 8-tops at lunchtime, Abe greeted guests with an enthusiastic, "Good afternoon."

The kitchen steward blocked his path. He was trying to stack the illegal 16 dishes onto his tray to serve both of his tables in one fell swoop again.

He was removing four plates when Arthur Winarick walked by and said, "Beckman and Pransky have already booked three acts for us."

Overhearing that, something twisted in his gut.

"What happens if Hershel slinks in here with his tail between his legs and wants his job back?" asked Irving.

"He's already let me down," Arthur said.

He steadied his tray in the air. If his bosses were not too worried that Hershel was being held against his will, then he would not worry too much either. Although something seemed fishy.

Dotty passed by carrying a single bowl of red Jell-O, and he reached his hand out toward her. She flinched, and he hooked his arm around her waist, preventing her from tripping. She froze in his embrace, and he breathed in her fragrant perfume. Bewildered by her skittishness, he sidestepped in the hope that she would divulge why she was in such a state.

"You startled me. My nerves are on high alert."

He raised his eyebrows.

She checked all corners of the room before meeting his eye. "D.R. grabbed me."

"Did he hurt you?" He flexed his muscles, ready to fight.

"No, but he ransacked my room and scared me."

He clenched his jaw. He wanted to deck the unwelcome visitor.

She darted her eyes at the door. Then she whispered, "Eva needs to disclose where she moved his money, along with Jack Drucker's money."

He was speechless for only a few seconds. "Eva had Drucker's money?"

"I've said too much. *Oy vey.*" She gazed at the Jell-O, shaking her dishwater-blonde hair.

A lightbulb went off. That's why he and Hershel could not find the money. All the cash Eva had with her last night and the Ford Deluxe she was driving around now made sense.

"*Oy vey,*" she repeated and pursed her lips. "Forget what you've just heard."

He watched her scuttle away for a moment longer. He was grateful she had been friendly and trusted him. He would like to invite her out for an egg cream one afternoon soon—and this time he would not stand her up. His shoulders were tense. His mind raced. And then alarm bells went off behind him.

"Call an ambulance! He's having a heart attack! Is there a doctor in here?" shouted a guest, crouching on the ground to get a front-row view.

A man at one of Dotty's tables had rolled out of his seat and hit the floor with a thud.

"Did he croak?" A guest jumped up to see the action. His cold tomatoes landed in the lap of the guest next to him.

The guest, with tomato-soiled clothing, dumped the breadbasket over their seatmate's head. As they threw punches, Abe positioned himself between the two. The dining room captain hurried over with a mixture in a milkshake glass and leaned down so the guest on the floor could take a sip.

All the guests expressed concern, acting as if it were one of their family members, holding their hands over their hearts.

"It's mountain magic," Eva told him, pointing at the milkshake glass.

The guest experienced a remarkable recovery on the spot. "He ate too much food. It wasn't a heart attack after all. It was a case of impaction," announced Irving.

"You'd be surprised at how many guests the simple mix of prune juice and hot water with a squeeze of lemon cures," Eva further explained.

He clapped his hands together, congratulating the guest's good fortune that it was not more serious.

Chaos was still ensuing at his table. The activity director saved him. He told the guest who had spilled the tomatoes onto the other guest's lap, "We're moving you to a superior seat."

The other guest bared his teeth. "Why was he given the better seat instead of me?"

Abe did his best to placate every single person at his tables. He developed a charley horse and took a moment to massage his calf. Waitresses sped past him, busboys rushed about, and guests shoveled food into their mouths and ordered more. He rolled his ankle around and transformed back into waiter mode. He had tips to earn.

Dotty had her tray held high. He tried to communicate without words, and she seemed to understand he was asking if she was all right by the gentle nod of her head.

The guests finally vacated the dining room. He was drying the last of the forks when Arthur, misty-eyed, reached an arm out. "Abe," he said in a tender tone. "I'm sorry."

Confused, he assumed that Arthur thought he was related to the guest with the impaction.

"It's your brother."

"Al or Norman?" he whispered, his mouth dry and his heart pounding against his chest.

"Al."

He collapsed to his knees. "I have to get home immediately."

Arthur patted his back. "May Al's memory be for a blessing. I've already arranged for a luxury car to drive you there. We'll hold your spot for you. Take all the time you need."

Everything was a blur as he sped off in a silver Rolls Royce.

CHAPTER 21
Week 2, Thursday

DOTTY

Dotty held the letter mailed from home. She could not, under any circumstances, withdraw from City College for her freshman year in the fall. So much for staying in the mountains after the season ended. She picked up her pencil with a heavy heart and a frown. Papa's dedication to daily prayers was why she was writing to him. She requested that he say an extra special prayer for Abe's brother, Al. The door opened and slammed against the wall, startling the wits right out of her.

"There's been a new talent booker team hired," Eva said with her hands on her head. She paced between their beds.

"*Oy vey*." Dotty shook her head and dropped her pencil. "You must straighten things out."

"I didn't mean for Hershel to lose his job. He'll go mad once he finds out Arthur has already replaced him with Beckman and Pransky."

"Hand over the money and sell the car. Make things right."

Eva parted the curtains and stared out at the greenery.

"You can end this, Eva. Please." She bit her tongue instead of admitting that she had witnessed Leon with his arms around Eva at the pool.

Eva tied the silky taupe scarf around her hair. "Come, let's go." She threw the Prussian blue scarf at Dotty.

"Where are we going? We have to be back for

dinner." She chased Eva through the hallway to the leveled land.

"Here, kitty, kitty," called Eva.

"What are you doing calling for Boychik?"

"Perhaps he'll bring us another piece of potential evidence?"

Achoo. She walked around and moved a pile of twigs with her foot. She saw a matchbook peeking out from the dirt. The tiny picture of the moon shining over trees stared back at her. Every Tom, Dick, and Harry must have a free matchbook from the sundry shop, so it puzzled her that her stomach was in an instant knot.

After another minute of calling for the cat with no response, Eva trekked on, leading Dotty to the fancy red convertible. "Hop in," Eva said.

The Ford Deluxe had a way of transforming her into a budding movie star in an instant. Dotty slipped into her sunglasses, tied the blue scarf around her hair, and was filled with questions as they headed west.

ABE

The wooden Coney Island Cyclone roller coaster plunged down the steep track in Steeplechase Park. He watched the passengers scream, standing outside the entrance, longing to turn the clock back to a Saturday night years ago. Once the Sabbath had ended, Al had surprised Abe, Norman, and Jean with tickets to the amusement park. Tears sprang to his eyes; it had been a perfect evening.

A Bing Crosby rendition floated through the air as he took a panoramic scan of the area. He lingered on the Wonder Wheel because the last time he had ridden the Ferris wheel, he had shared a seat with Al. They had both been in awe of the view from the top. Afterward, they raced each other to Nathan's Famous, where they ate scrumptious frankfurters. Then they ventured onto the Parachute Jump, which some people called the "Eiffel Tower of Brooklyn."

Today he ate at the frankfurter stand alone. He missed his older brother, who had died when a Japanese sniper shot him while he was setting up communications on one of the Pacific islands.

He observed a man handing out frankfurters like it was a magic trick. One after the other would appear in his hand, and within seconds the man dispersed them all to the hungry crowd. Abe had never seen anything like it anywhere but here. To his left, Nathan Handwerker, a Jewish immigrant from Russia, watched his restaurant like a hawk. He sold the Depression-era crowd superior beef franks. The lines were long, but they moved at a swift pace. The men behind the counter had a system—they collected nickel after nickel as the frankfurters cooked on the grill.

He applied *schmears* of mustard to his frankfurter from the big metal bowl on the counter at Nathan's Famous. In his mind, he heard Al say, "The secret spices are the talk of the boardwalk." It was a hot, summery Friday afternoon. He stood on the boardwalk, eating and watching the Atlantic Ocean. He wondered where in the universe Al existed now, if anywhere at all. The waves crashed onto the shore, and he sank into a deep memory from long ago.

An unfamiliar suitcase sat by the door of his childhood home; a pink satin ribbon was tied around the handle.

"Abe-ala, put on your shoes," Ma had snapped at him. "Al and Norman are already outside."

"Where are we going?"

Ma had ignored his question and called for Jean.

He had touched the handle of the suitcase. "I'm hungry." His stomach had growled.

"Let's go!" Ma had Jean in her arms, so she had knocked the screen door open with her hip. "The taxicab is coming."

He had shoved his feet into his shoes; his right toe poked through a hole in the front. He had told Ma he needed new ones. Confused and hungry, he had worn them anyway.

"Come, kinder, get in," Ma had snapped again.

"Ow," he cried out as his head hit the yellow taxicab door. Ma pushed him onto the seat as Jean sobbed and clung to her.

A dreadful lump inside his stomach overpowered the hunger pains as Ma pried Jean's tiny fingers away from her neck and flung her onto the seat beside him.

Al had yelled out, "Why are you sending us off, Ma?"

"I'm going to Chicago to start a new life."

The driver was impatient and had asked for the address and fare. Ma had reached into her pocket and recited Papa's address. Usually, she accompanied them to the apartment building.

Jean had crawled onto Al's lap while Abe and Norman sat stunned into silence. The screech of tires and the smell of hot rubber marked the four siblings' permanent departure from the only home they had ever known. Abe had pressed his nose against the window.

He had wanted to keep Ma in sight as long as possible. Watching her dance up the steps so merrily at sending them away had made him sad. As the taxicab neared its destination, the driver looked at Abe with sympathetic eyes.

All 5 feet 3 inches of Papa had hurried toward them from the end of the block. There had been a brief moment when Al and Abe had stood alone. "I don't want to live in an orphanage," Abe had said.

Al had put his arms around his younger brother. "I promise I'll keep you safe."

The next morning over a bowl of fruit salad for breakfast, Papa said, "You're going to Bubbe and Zayde's house. We should hold your mother's family responsible since your mother has brought all the trouble to us."

The months had rolled on and Bubbe continued to fill the maternal role. On Yom Kippur, Papa had arrived with a live chicken. Abe had stared at the poultry, craving it. Other than Rosh Hashanah, they had not had a meal like that in ages. When Papa swung the chicken over Abe's head, saying prayers, the loud voices started.

"It's too much! We've been feeding your kinder for a year. We're exhausted!" Bubbe had shouted.

"Genug iz genug," Zayde had said. "We can't do it anymore."

Jean and Norman had bawled beside him, and Abe, with a trembling lip, had turned to Al like he always had. His big brother repeated the same line from a year before: "I promise I'll keep you safe."

The reassurance was what Abe had needed. His

brother had known it.

The crowd cheering over someone catching a flounder pulled his attention back to the present. His heart swelled with tremendous love for his older brother. Without Al alive, he was the eldest and regarded that duty with deep responsibility. The sign for the freak show, where people with abnormalities performed, choked him up. He and Al had always talked about attending a show. His feet were heavy as he walked east in the direction of Brighton Beach.

DOTTY

"You know how I admitted that I moved the money that D.R. is determined to get his hands on?" Eva took a sharp turn and the wind whipped at their faces. "Well, I reburied it near the haystacks by the pond and we're going to dig it up."

Eva handed Dotty a piece of paper. "See where the X is? That's where we are going."

She unfolded the hand-drawn map and began to pray they would not encounter any gangsters.

Eva tilted her head to the left. "That's Jack Drucker's farm."

Acres of farmland, with herds of cows and sheep, rolled by. Nothing appeared menacing, though the article she had read said otherwise.

"How many dead bodies do you think he has buried on his land?" asked Eva.

Chills ran up and down her spine. She stared straight ahead as Eva wound this way and that, took a left there, and then a right after that. She would never be able to find her way out on her own. The car came to a stop between haystacks and a small pond.

"We're here." Eva held a hand shovel and leaped from the convertible. She did not waste a second racing underneath a maple tree and kneeling to pat the earth.

Dotty bit the inside of her cheek and paused to check out the surroundings. She saw a car coming their way.

Eva crouched down, hiding behind a tree trunk. She pulled Dotty down with her. "That's Hershel's oldest brother. I don't want them to know I'm out here," she whispered.

The maroon Cadillac turned onto a path near a forest of trees. Eva stood up and circled the area. "I know it was right here."

"Why did you move it?"

"So Drucker's Rat can't get his hands on it. I told Hershel that burying it near the apple orchard and the chicken coop wasn't smart. The spot was too obvious. I thought it should be in a more desolate area. He didn't agree, so I moved it on my own."

She removed the Prussian blue scarf. Staring at a family of ducklings swimming across the pond, she said another prayer. Then she hurried over beside Eva, who was jabbing the hand shovel into the dirt.

"Before his disappearance, Hershel had been trying to get in touch with Jack Drucker to see if D.R.'s story held up. I think Hershel deserves a nice sum for helping Jack avoid losing it all to the authorities." Eva threw shovels of dirt over her shoulder.

"Does D.R. suspect you moved the money?"

"No, but he assumed Hershel would've told me where he buried it. On the night of the fire, D.R. drove me over here and insisted that I reveal exactly where the money was buried. While I was stranded here, I dug a fake hole next to the chicken coop just to mislead him."

A burst of wind blew through the trees. Eva's silky taupe scarf came loose and fluttered through the air. Dotty caught it.

"Aren't we lucky I had the foresight to move the money," Eva said as a mourning dove hovered overhead. She dug another couple of inches into the ground, grunting.

Dotty moved rocks aside. Eva dug faster until she dropped her shovel to the ground and started tugging a metal safe out of the earth. Her unkempt hair was hanging in her face. Her filthy hands scratched at the lid. "It's stuck."

"Don't you need to know the code?"

"The lock has already been broken. Get out of the way." Eva held a sharp rock over her head.

She lunged to the side and covered her ears. The rock slammed into the metal. After three more hits, the lid of the safe popped wide open. "This is a fortune," she gasped, her eyes bugging out.

"That's why we're keeping a little more." Eva stuffed dollar bills into her handbag.

"I think you've swiped enough already." Her nerves jumped like an acrobat on a Ringling Brothers trampoline. She pictured the money Eva had stuffed under her mattress. "Can we leave now?"

Eva scooped the safe into her arms, loaded it into the car, and sped out of there. Dirt went flying from the skid of the tires. "Don't worry, I'll have us back in time for dinner."

She did not doubt that for a second with the rate

of speed at which they were traveling. "When are you handing over the money?"

Eva kept her eyes on the road ahead and sang "Just as Though You Were Here" by Frank Sinatra.

She hummed along. It was rather nice to take a drive through farmland in such a swanky car. If only it had not been under such stressful circumstances.

Eva slammed the brakes near the boat docks at Kiamesha Lake and ran to a mossy spot behind a patch of oak trees, carrying the safe. Dotty grabbed the hand shovel, took one big, deep breath, and followed. She waited a moment to exhale before kneeling to help. Eva was digging rocks out of the way with her hands.

"Why aren't you handing the money over instead of burying it again? This better not be because you want to spend more time with Leon. Eva, you have to free Hershel," she implored.

Eva grunted and snatched the shovel out of her hands.

"It's an osprey nest!" shouted a voice behind the oak trees.

Eva threw pebbles, dirt, and sticks aside.

"Ospreys are big hawks," said a voice that sounded way too close.

Dotty squatted again and, holding her breath, helped Eva ease the safe into the earth. She was green around the gills as they scraped dirt over the safe and reburied it.

A voice said, "We better hurry and change for dinner."

Eva wiped dirt from her watch and beseeched Dotty to get to the shoreline. "Wash up and fast!"

She removed her shoes before splashing lake water onto her arms and face. Huffing and puffing, they sprinted to the hotel. She waved a quick hello as they passed by the sundry shop where Marv was in the entryway, pacing. He looked tousled and lacked his navy vest. Then she waved to the evening porter. Finally, she waved at Sy, rushing down the hallway, his hands in his pockets and his gaze straight ahead. It seemed important to get the button back that she had given to him, but there was no time.

They undressed and made it to dinner in their uniforms as the first guests arrived. She mouthed a gigantic thank you to her busboy for preparing the tables alone. Her eyes rested on a monkey dish. The knot of sympathy she had been carrying for Abe ached.

The man who had suffered from impaction earlier ordered a single entrée. She was pleased to see him sticking with a portion that did not make him ill.

Irving strutted by, grinning like the Cheshire Cat. He led two sharp-dressed men through the dining room.

Eva leaned into her right ear, "That's Albert Beckman and Johnny Pransky."

The shorter of the two men spoke up. "There's a rumor that Sophie Tucker might make a surprise visit to the mountains."

The taller one winked. "We will guarantee the Concord is her first stop."

Starstruck, Dotty's eyes caught the bulky notebook each man held. Under her breath, she mumbled, "They didn't miss a beat replacing

Hershel."

"I think it's time I speak with Arthur about Hershel's connection with Jack Drucker," Eva admitted. A saltshaker rolled off her server stand.

Dotty hopped two feet off the ground when it crashed to the ground.

CHAPTER 22
Week 3, Friday

ABE

"What are the odds someone has murdered him?" Irving asked.

Back in the mountains and at work, Abe lingered outside the doorway. His stomach hollowed as he waited for Arthur's response.

"It's Hershel—he's like a cat with nine lives."

"You've gone and hired Beckman and Pransky. Even if Hershel slinks back in with his tail between his legs, he doesn't have a job here anymore," Irving pointed out.

He balled his hands into fists and knocked twice on Irving's door.

"Come in." Irving waved him into his office and stood up to shake his hand with a gentle grip. A cigar was dangling from his lips.

Arthur extended his hand next. "I was listening to the radio, and my wheels started turning. Once the men are home from the army, I want to hold a Jewish War Veterans convention here. We'll put out all the bells and whistles. They deserve it. I'll tell the chef to make the best matzo ball soup anyone has ever tasted. I want all the Jewish veterans and refugees on my staff to be part of it. I have a vision of holding lots of conventions." Arthur tightened his grip on Abe's hand. "We'll honor your brother in some significant way."

"That's a great idea, Boss." Touched, he bowed his head.

Irving leaned back in his chair and puffed on his

cigar. "You're a real *mensch,* Abe."

Arthur cleared his throat. "I only hire the best at my hotel. That's why we've decided to promote you. If you're ready for the added responsibility."

He went ahead and prematurely nodded "yes."

"How would you like to run the staff dining room?"

His heart beat faster.

Irving plucked the cigar out of his mouth to say, "It's a big job, and it offers steady, all-season work."

His lips flickered into a smile. He was flattered; it was the first spark of joy he had experienced since learning of Al's death.

Irving added, "Important folks like to eat in there. Arthur eats every meal there since no dress code is required. We'll ask Leon to go in as a co-captain with you. I knew you two were lightning rods since the first time I laid eyes on you both."

Arthur winked. "I like my eggs on the runny side."

Irving shifted in his chair. "Rumor has it that the dining room staff may hold a secret vote on unions soon."

He had heard no such thing himself, yet he had just returned. "My vote will be against it," he told his bosses, meaning it.

"Thank you, Abe. That's what I like to hear. If a union comes here, I want it legit, not run by gangsters," Arthur said.

"Now go stick your head inside the staff dining room to get a lay of the land. If you see Leon, send him my way," Irving said with a friendly smile.

Eva burst into the office as Abe was *schlepping* his bag back over his shoulder, astonished at his good fortune. She thrust a notebook into Arthur's hands. "There's information you need to know regarding Hershel."

He stood near the doorway, listening instead of exiting.

Arthur clutched Hershel's talent booking notebook to his chest. "I do miss the guy. It's not the same around here without him."

Eva ran her eyes from Arthur to Irving. "I think you need to contact Jack Drucker."

"Drucker's in prison!" Irving yelled.

"What is Hershel mixed up in?" asked Arthur, peering down at Hershel's handwriting. His posture was tense as he flipped through the pages.

Eva tucked her curls behind her ears. "He could be in real trouble."

He tightened his hold on his bag and narrowed his eyes. His brother's death had made him forget all about what Dotty had let slip about D.R. and Drucker's money. As Arthur and Irving were firing off questions, he slipped away without drawing attention. The memory of the maroon Cadillac was nagging at him. Perhaps he would sneak back over to Hershel's farm later and nose around for clues to his pal's current location.

He went to scope out his new spot of employment. Appreciation filled his heart as he envisioned all the entertainers he would get to meet. He counted 10 tables in the empty staff dining room, the majority of which were four-tops. He had dropped out of high school before graduation, and here he was advancing so quickly, serving the big shots all their meals. An urge to write to his older brother, who had always been his greatest champion, prompted a wave of grief over the impossibility of speaking with him ever again. Lightheaded, he leaned against the closest wall to regain his composure.

Leon charged into the staff dining room. "Abe! A real opportunity has been given to us."

"You aren't kidding."

They shook hands and bumped shoulders.

DOTTY

Between lunch and dinner, Dotty was watching a game of Simon Says when she caught sight of Abe. "You're back so soon?"

"Hello, Dot."

"What about *shiva*?" She presumed he would stay in Brooklyn through the weekend to observe the seven-day Jewish mourning period after his brother's funeral.

He patted his heart. "I know Al is here with me. I decided the best thing would be to throw myself into work. I didn't want to leave Irving short for Shabbat dinner."

Impressed by his work ethic, she reached out and wrapped her arms around him. He returned the hug and even added a squeeze. She did not mind at all. It was pleasant to rest against his broad chest as the salty smell of ocean water permeated her nostrils.

"I hear there has been no word from Hershel."

"No," she said, disappointed that their embrace had to end so soon.

He changed the position of the bag hanging over his shoulder. "There's still time for him to be at the show."

She did not point out that even if he resurfaced by then, he no longer had his job. Now that Abe was standing in more direct light, she could see the black rings under his eyes. "If there's anything I can do to help you through your loss, don't hesitate to ask."

"Thank you, Dot. Al was a real fine fellow. It's a shame you didn't get to meet him."

She, too, wished she had a chance to meet Abe's older brother.

He opened his mouth as if he had something important to say, but he was interrupted by a chef who wanted to offer his condolences. She waved goodbye and went to rest her feet in anticipation of a hectic Friday night dinner.

Before taking a catnap in her bed, she moved a chair in front of the door as she had been doing ever since Drucker's Rat had snatched her. She shut her eyes, falling into a dream centered around Abe.

CHAPTER 23

ABE

Abe lifted a table above his head as Irving strode into the staff dining room. Leon stopped humming and whispered, "Are you going to ask him about the quarters?"

Amid dinner preparation, an idea had taken root, and he had shared it with Leon. He figured he might as well get it over with right away. "Say, Boss, I have an idea I would like to run by you."

"All right, go ahead."

"We'd like to be tipped in here, like the waiters in the main dining room. Our proposal is a quarter after every meal."

"That's a clever request. It sounds reasonable to tip two hard workers a quarter. I don't think it will ruffle any feathers," Irving agreed.

Abe, wearing his dinner jacket, bow tie, and black pants ensemble, stepped forward and shook his boss's hand. Then he placed four chairs around the table.

Arthur entered the room, his face hanging heavy as he sat down. Abe poured a cold pitcher of water into Arthur's glass. He overheard him telling Irving, "I can't find any credible news about Hershel. It was a lucky break that the prison warden stayed at Grossinger's and was fond of the area, so he answered my call. He wasn't able to put me on the phone with Drucker."

"Hershel takes great pride in his work. He wouldn't intentionally miss Danny's show tomorrow, but with each passing hour, I'm losing confidence," said Irving. He was sitting at the table behind Arthur's.

"It's a good thing I went ahead and hired those acclaimed talent bookers," Arthur said before perking back up. "The shows must go on. Prepare for Sophie Tucker to eat in here next week."

"My ma loves Sophie Tucker for how risqué she is," Abe said. He was considering a trip to Hershel's farm after dinner.

"I heard her on the radio with Milton Berle," Leon added.

"Al once told me about watching Milton Berle perform for his troop overseas and how much he enjoyed the show." He pulled out a chair and sat in it.

Leon placed a hand on his shoulder. "Won't that be something when he performs at the Concord and eats in here?"

He shook off the grief and led Marv, the shopkeeper, to a two-top. "What can I start you off with this evening?"

"Just a bowl of soup, please," he said, his kind blue eyes bloodshot.

"Been hard at work selling Jeris?" Abe teased.

Marv mumbled about losing track of something important and searching for it; Abe could not quite hear.

Moss Hart, the celebrated playwright and theater director, arrived, and he hurried over to lead him to Arthur's table. Moss spent his vacation eating in the staff dining room to avoid being disturbed by the guests.

The best way to combat his grief was by working and staying busy. He listened to their banter, impressed by Arthur's ability to carry on a conversation about absolutely anything.

While delivering a baked potato to Moss Hart, he overheard him tell Arthur, at the four-top across from him, "I hope you'll see *Dear Ruth* during its run on Broadway." Arthur was eating anchovies.

Abe had never been to a Broadway production. He was imagining attending his first one when Alexander Olshanetsky interrupted him.

"Can I please have some more of the delicious stuffed cabbage?" asked the Yiddish composer, who led the orchestra at the Concord.

He retrieved the desired dish. Upon his return, Moss Hart held a gorgeous emerald-green, sequined, floor-length gown and a golden, mermaid-sleeved, floor-length gown.

"I trust you two will make sure I get the end cut of the prime rib on Saturday night." To seal the deal, I'll give you these gowns." The playwright thrust one into Abe's hands and the other into Leon's.

Irving shuffled over to inspect them. "Do you want it for your wife, Boss? The other one can go to Arthur's wife." Abe extended the emerald-green gown to him.

Leon, admiring the golden gown, raised his head to see Irving's response. Irving touched the green material with his thumb. "Looks like a talented seamstress put her mark on it."

"The gowns were made for a scene in *Dear Ruth*. The costume designers wanted to go in another direction," Moss Hart explained.

"Take someone special to the Ratner for Mambo Night tonight," Alexander Olshanetsky volunteered. "Tell them I sent you."

He scratched his ear. He thought Mambo Night at the Ratner was on Monday nights, not on a Friday night.

"It's usually every Monday, after their hotel gigs when the area's best Latin musicians play at the Ratner," Alexander said as if he could hear Abe's internal monologue. "But I happen to know there is a special jam session there tonight."

He said a buoyant, "thank you," for permission to use such a renowned musician's name at one of the most well-known hotels. The Ratner was right down the hill from the Concord. As he waited to see if Irving wanted the gown, a faraway look crossed his face. He knew his big brother would have enjoyed such an event.

Arthur piped into the conversation. "Mambo Night is a sight to behold. The Latin bands will knock your socks off. You'll be tangoing until the sun comes up."

"You're already learning that running a dining room offers nice perks. Keep the dresses, but don't be late to serve breakfast in the morning," warned Irving, holding his glass out for a refill.

He put the gown aside and retrieved a water pitcher. He knew it was Dotty he wanted to invite to Mambo Night. A burst of energy surged through him, envisioning her wiggling her hips in the elegant gown. He knew without a doubt who Leon wanted to be the receiver of the golden gown.

Irving ripped open a rose-colored envelope. "It's another wedding invitation. I orchestrated this courtship by sitting the bride next to the groom during the High Holidays." He winked and held a tasteful ivory invitation in the air for his tablemates, the head of maintenance and the head plumber, to admire.

The head plumber called out for more stuffed cabbage as Abe spotted a figure in the doorway. He hissed at the gangster, "We don't want any trouble."

D.R. flared his nostrils and pointed at Leon. "Send him out to have a word with me."

Determined to keep the peace, he followed the instructions. He ran a one-man show while Leon talked to the unwanted visitor.

Arthur requested dessert, then said, "I spent the afternoon listening to Olshanetsky's recital. They performed pieces by Beethoven and Tchaikovsky."

"He has undeniable musical talent," Abe said, trying to maintain a sprightly voice even if his stomach was a lump of unease. Out of the corner of his eye, he saw Leon pause in the doorway. He grabbed the empty breadbasket. "I'll go get more," he told the table and dove over to Leon's side.

"If Eva doesn't hand over what he's searching for immediately, severe action will be taken," Leon whispered and gripped a yellow cat collar in his hands.

He swallowed hard. Dotty had told him in confidence that Eva had reburied Drucker's money; it was not his secret to reveal, so he leaped forward with the breadbasket. He did not want anything to interfere with tonight's mambo night. He vowed to start poking around for more information about where the money was hidden tomorrow.

DOTTY

Dotty caught sight of Leon holding a glamorous golden gown in the air, careful not to drag it on the floor. A busboy next to her was coughing, and a dishwasher yelled out, "A spoonful of Southern Comfort will cure your cold right up!"

The next time she felt under the weather, she might give that remedy a try. Her curiosity landed back on the gown Leon was carrying and the disturbed expression on his face. Not surprised to see him take a shortcut to Eva, she searched for Abe and fiddled with the Shabbat candlesticks.

Eva stopped at her station. "Oh, what have I done?" Her face crumpled.

"Has there been news?" She pressed a hand to her heart.

"No news." Eva blinked away tears.

"What has happened then?"

"I need to distance myself from Leon to keep him safe. D.R. threatened him and might've harmed Boychik," Eva reached for her necklace, but it was no longer there.

Her jaw tensed. An unhinged Eva on the job was out of character. She saw Irving *schmoozing* with a rabbi, glad he was missing Eva's meltdown. Because work came first, her follow-up questions had to go on the back burner. They had tables to finish setting up for dinner in a hurry. Eva fluffed her hair with her fingers, threw back her shoulders, and voilà, she was in professional mode.

Dotty scanned the dining room to see if Leon still had the golden gown hanging over his arm. She tried to pinpoint Abe's movements again, figuring Irving was going easy on him since he was mourning his older brother.

The guests were prompt, and the whirlwind began. A male shouted out, "I need matzo ball soup!" He plunked down and bit ravenously into a braided challah.

It was no surprise that everyone else wanted matzo ball soup, too. Right outside the kitchen, she hit the brakes next to Eva. "Where are Abe and Leon?"

"You didn't hear about their promotion?"

Eva pushed through the kitchen doors as she shouted, "Tell me!"

Eva boxed the other waitress out with her elbows and loaded her tray. Dotty grabbed bowls of soup.

A plate clanked to the floor behind them, and a cluster of activity broke out, causing Dotty to lose Eva in the commotion. She had no choice but to hurry back to her station. She heard her name, and her eyes landed on a sequined emerald-green gown dangling in the air.

"Ta-da!" Abe presented it to her as if he had designed it for the Queen of England.

She wiped her hands on her apron before tracing her fingers over the sequins and appliqué fabric. "Where did this come from?"

He cleared his throat. "It's a perk of my new job."

"Tell me!"

"You're looking at the co-captain of the staff dining room. Leon's the other one."

"Co-captain of the staff dining room is a big deal, Abe!"

"It's a year-round position! I'll be staying in the mountains for every season."

His advance tickled her. He had the privilege of waiting on all the entertainers who performed at the hotel. She was jealous that he would not have to pack his bags and head home after Labor Day.

"How would you like to go dancing at the Ratner tonight?"

Stunned by the invite, she squealed, "Oh, the Ratner!"

He dropped his voice. "Alexander Olshanetsky gave me permission to use his name at the special jam session there later."

"A personal invite to a special jam session!" she fluttered her eyelashes at him.

A woman passed by and reached for his arm. "I have a granddaughter back in Brooklyn who's coming to the Concord next weekend. That dress is her size. Why don't you save it for her and show her a good time?"

She wanted Abe to tell the woman to get lost, but knowing he would never treat a guest with such disrespect, she just stood there, gritting her teeth.

"It's all yours, Dot." He pinched her side. She melted and beamed at the beauty.

He beamed right back until Irving called him over. Eva stood in his place and touched a finger to the emerald-green gown. "Abe's a full-timer now. Do you know what life is like here after Labor Day?"

She shook her head with reluctance.

"It's vastly different from what it is in the summer. Everyone is trying to survive the long, cold winter together under the same roof. Steamy hookups and short-lived romances are the norm. Competing egos, personality conflicts, and the occasional fistfight keep things interesting."

A pit formed in her stomach. "It sounds like it's exciting no matter the season. Just because a lot of fellas do that stuff all winter long, it doesn't mean Abe will be philandering about." The strawberry-blonde-haired dancer's face floated in the air.

Eva gave her a long look. "I turned down Leon's invitation."

"If you aren't going to Mambo Night, neither will I." *Would the cook who suggested Southern Comfort for an illness also recommend it for a disappointed heart?*

ABE

"What do you say we go to Mambo Night, just the two of us?" Abe asked. He held a pair of cuff links.

Leon sighed, placing the yellow cat collar with great care into a paper bag, treating it like evidence.

He knew his friend was not up for it. Still, he squeezed a drop of Jeris Hair Tonic into his hands and rubbed it into his hair. Unsure of what had caused Dotty to cancel, he was trying to shake off his disappointment. The answer she had given him was vague about needing to do something with Eva. Now his original plan of going out to Hershel's farm after dinner was an option again. There was a knock at the door, and he slicked his hair back in a hurry. "Maybe they changed their minds." He swung the door open.

"My feet ache. I left my coin purse at my station. Which one of you can go retrieve it for me?" Betty asked. She had ace bandages wrapped around her wrists ever since returning from her couple of days off when Abe had become a waiter himself.

"I'd be happy to help you out." He shut his eyes

and for a moment let himself believe he was getting ready to race his brothers. "Growing up I won every relay race around the block. I was the most athletic of my brothers. In high school, they wanted me to play football," he told Leon before sprinting off.

He reached the dining room in record time. At the server stand, he found the coin purse that had fallen to the ground and was startled to hear a female voice cry out and even more startled to hear a busboy's voice he recognized.

He found what he had come for and disappeared from the room. Embarrassed to have interrupted the secret tryst, he decided he would not share what he had accidentally heard with anyone.

After returning the purse, he was headed to his room when Dotty sashayed toward him in the emerald-green gown. "*Shayna!*" he called, his eyes ogling at the fair amount of cleavage exposed. The cinched waist hugged her hips and enhanced her figure.

"I couldn't miss the opportunity to wear such a perfect gown." She twirled once in front of him. Her dangling mercury-dime earrings sparkled under the light.

Verklempt, he inhaled her floral-scented perfume—she was *farpitst*. He reached for her hand and kissed it. More click-clacking of high heels came closer, and he turned to see Eva. She was a sight for sore eyes as well.

Leon popped out of their room. "*Shayna!*" he exclaimed at the sight of his date, his cheeks rosy, and his sadness lifted in that moment.

Eva curtsied and then half-frowned. "I wish I had

my special opal heart-shaped necklace as an accessory."

Abe knew that each time Leon passed a jewelry case, he stopped to see if there was anything like Eva's stolen necklace. So far, there had been nothing.

Eva smacked her lips together and made an announcement. "I'm driving to the Ratner. Tomorrow, I'm selling the convertible. I'll make everything right."

Leon stuck his arm out, and Eva grabbed onto it. Abe put his hand on the small of Dotty's back. He led her outside, where mating frogs and chirping crickets serenaded them.

As he was settling into the backseat, Eva tooted her horn. "Watch out, Marv," she yelled at the sundry shop owner who was behind the wheel of a maroon Cadillac.

Abe's eyes bulged. *That's the exact Cadillac model I saw the night of the fire right when Hershel went missing.* But as soon as they were cruising down the mountain in style, his sole focus was on dancing the night away with Dotty. They got past the security gatekeeper by dropping Alexander's name and acting as if they belonged. He held Dotty's hand as they waltzed through the hotel lobby to the dance floor, which sizzled with energy. An ensemble of jazz musicians played their hearts out.

The crowd, in flamboyant attire, mamboed in every direction. Abe, careful not to bump into any of the mamboing couples, kept contact with Dotty as they wiggled their way into an inch of free floor space. She shook her *tuchus* to the beat as he threw his head back and stepped in rhythm with her.

A conga line formed. Dotty held onto the person's shoulders in front of her and swung her hips. He danced behind her, circling the exterior of the showroom.

Not until the third set did he take a break to gulp water. He watched Leon try some intricate footwork as Dotty used the washroom. Usually, Leon was a dead hoofer. He could not stop chuckling until someone slapped him on the back. He spun around. "Sy! Nice to see you."

"I've been wanting to speak with you, kid."

He was all ears, but the intensity of the music increased, making it impossible to carry on a conversation. Dotty snaked back through the crowd to his side.

"Hi, sweetheart. Your dress fits you like a glove." Sy raised a bottle of amber beer in the air.

Her cheeks flushed at the compliment.

Sy tipped his beer in Eva and Leon's direction. "There seems to be quite a bit of two-timing going on. Hershel might very well be shacking up with a different waitress as we speak." Sy chugged from his beer and wiped his mouth with his wrist.

Abe liked the thought of that over some of the possibilities, although he did not consider it likely.

The bandleader from Esther Manor sat down in front of a drum set. The beat was low. It grew louder as the drummer from Lesser Lodge joined the acoustic set. They were competing to see who would get the most applause.

Sy cleared his throat and leaned into his right ear. "I've watched you gamble quite a few times now. You've got the smarts and the determination my investment club requires to be a member. How would you like to attend our next meeting?"

He could not imagine why Sy would want someone as far down on the totem pole as he was, but he sure did want to say "yes."

"We're looking for some young spitfires." Sy slapped him on the back. "What do you say, kid? Do you want to do some investing?"

Dotty was right there, so he knew it was best to remain noncommittal. He was glad the music kept her attention off Sy.

"All right, kid. I'll catch up with you another time to discuss important business." Sy raised his beer to his lips and disappeared into the crowd.

Dotty furrowed her eyebrows and leaned into his ear. "Is he here for Drucker's money?"

He put his arm around her waist. "Seems like he's here to enjoy himself like the rest of us." He could tell she was not convinced by the way she was darting her eyes around the room.

"I won't tell him where it is now buried."

"Pardon?" A jam session with 10 to 15 musicians playing lit the place up. The skilled instrumentalist from the Heiden Hotel was stealing the show. It made it impossible to hear Dotty. He could see her lips moving in a perturbed state.

Eva and Leon smooching caught his attention. "I'd better tell my co-captain to call it a night unless I want to run the staff dining room all by myself in the morning." He needed Leon by his side for breakfast.

"I wish the night didn't have to end."

"Don't worry, Dot. We'll have many more nights

like this. I'm not going anywhere."

He tapped her nose with his finger. "You look like a kid who had her balloon stolen. The summer fantasy is far from over; it's just the beginning."

"You're in fine spirits because you're accustomed to constant change, and you get to stay here all year long. The thought of leaving the mountains at the end of the summer makes me melancholy." She stuck out her bottom lip.

"Why not ask Irving to hire you for all the seasons?"

"Papa would never allow that. He made me promise I'd return for college."

He would rather have this conversation at a quieter time. "Stay put and I'll be right back with Eva and Leon." He cut through the crowd. After a lot of convincing, they left the dance floor. Eva excused herself to use the washroom, and he spun around. He locked eyes with Leon. "What are you going to do when Hershel returns?"

"*If* Hershel returns."

"*Oy vey*." He hoped Eva kept her word tomorrow as he traced his steps back to where he had left Dotty. "Where'd she go?" he asked the closest person in proximity to the exact spot where he had left his date. He did not think she could be far.

CHAPTER 24
Week 3, Saturday

DOTTY

Abe was very handsome with his hair slicked back with Jeris Hair Tonic. "Ouch," she cried, trying to pull her arm back. The calloused hand wrapped around her wrist hurt.

"You're coming with me," growled a gruff voice.

"Abe!" she yelled over the drummer from Esther Manor and the drummer from Lesser Lodge, who were in the middle of a duet.

The other calloused hand, with the chunky pinky ring, clenched around her mouth. She was dragged to the door in one swift move, kicking her feet and trying to scream.

Once they were in a dark hallway, the hand was released from her mouth and she gulped at air. Her right wrist was still held in a vice-like grip. She was tugged to a doorway with smoke billowing from underneath. Three men wearing tailored gray suits swaggered by. D.R. was manic, so she shut her lips and trembled instead of calling out to them. Goosebumps dotted her skin. She was taking short breaths, seconds away from vomiting into the tall birds of paradise in the corner. She was pushed through the door. Her gown caught on something, tearing the thread; sequins fell to the floor.

D.R. led her to a table under the brightest light. A man wearing striped suspenders slapped a stack of cash onto it. The last time she had seen that amount of money, it was trouble.

"Sit," directed D.R.

With great trepidation, she stuck her *tuchus* right onto the seat.

"Reveal where Eva hid the money, and you will go free."

She blinked several times and, gathering her courage, asked, "Will you also release Hershel?"

D.R. squinted. "You do know where the money is buried." He latched onto her wrist once again.

"Ouch." Tears sprang to the corners of her eyes as she was yanked into the air. Her heart was in her stomach as she willed Abe to rescue her.

Her kidnapper's pace was faster than she could handle in high heels. She stumbled and bumped into another man's side. The man's meaty fingers reached out to help steady her on her feet.

"Sy!" she yelled and tried to claw at his leg as D.R. picked her up and threw her over his shoulder. Her left mercury dime earring landed on the ground. "Tell Abe to meet me at the Kiamesha Lake boat docks!" The door slammed in her face. "Ouch," she cried out for the third time.

"Eva buried it at the lake, huh?" D.R. kept clicking his tongue.

Sure enough, once she was placed on the ground, she bent over and vomited. The chirps from the crickets were pulsing in her ears.

ABE

Abe wiped his brow, leaned against a wall, stretched his back, and rolled his neck around his shoulders. The Latin music was a constant beat in the background. Both confused and afraid, he could not think of a single reason that Dotty would have taken off on her own. An image of the emerald-green gown fluttering around her hips as she mamboed filled his mind.

He could use Eva and Leon's help, but they had dismissed his concern. They were back on the dance floor as he continued the hunt, racing up a wide hallway. A fella was coming at him, snapping his fingers to get his attention.

"You must get to Kiamesha Lake!" Sy shouted, catching his breath and holding one of Dotty's earrings in the air.

He came to a halt and gawked at him, confusion lining his face.

"Dotty gave me the message. I came here tonight to protect you. And the moment I was, ahem, answering nature's call, Dotty got snatched. Unbelievable." Sy shook his head. "Come, I'll drive you back to the Concord."

Unfamiliar with the Ratner's layout, he jogged beside Sy to the parking lot. He dove into the passenger seat of a black sedan, and off they sped. "Why did you think we needed protecting?"

Sy kept his foot heavy on the gas pedal. "As you know, I hear things. Today I learned that D.R. was planning on taking whoever he could to lead him to the buried money once and for all." They rounded the corner and cruised through the gates of the Concord.

Sy slammed the brakes. Abe threw himself out of the car. He held his hands straight out in front of him as he stumbled his way through the darkness toward the lake.

Was that a scream? He put his hand over his

thumping heart. "Dotty!" he yelled into the night. The crescent moon was peeking from behind the clouds. He ran closer to the shore.

A movement and rustling in the bushes alarmed him. "Dotty!" he shouted again. A critter lunged out of the bushes and he panicked, punching and kicking. A loud meow and the glimpse of gray fur caused his panic to simmer. "Boychik, is that you?"

Another meow that sounded like "yes" rang through the night air. He squinted at the cat and saw a speck of something gleaming in the moonlight. He crept closer and was able to make out emerald-green sequins stuck in Boychik's singed fur. "Dotty!" he yelled louder. Terrified for her, he hurtled himself into the night. A tree branch scratched the skin on his right cheek. He used the back of his hand to wipe the blood away. Boychik was flicking his tail, with a missing patch of fur, to the left.

He followed the cat until a deep voice said, "Stop right there."

His knees buckled at the sight of the revolver. He heard a whimper. "Dotty," he whispered, pivoting his head with caution, hyperaware of the gun aimed at his forehead. Fear surged through his body. Desperate to protect her, his eyes landed on the tip of the metal safe sticking out of the earth.

"Start digging," the gunman demanded.

He dropped to the earth and dug with his bare hands.

D.R. leered at Dotty and held the revolver steady. Her trembling body knocked into Abe's. "I'll keep you safe." He spoke the same words that had always reassured him when they came out of Al's mouth.

"Faster," snapped D.R.

Boychik snuck out of the nighttime shadows and bit his ankle, drawing blood.

"Ouch!" D.R. yelped. He swung the revolver around, targeting the cat, who had already vanished into the darkness.

Abe reached both of his hands into the hole and eased the metal safe free from the dirt. D.R. knocked him out of the way, yanking the lid open and sticking his nose inside.

He stood. He hoisted Dotty, wearing only one earring and her dirt-covered gown, up along with him. A loose thread caught on a stick, unraveling into a monkey dish-sized hole on the side of her waist; more green sequins landed in the dirt. "Let's get out of here," he whispered, clutching her hand tight.

D.R. blocked their path. "This is nowhere near the amount I'm owed. You two aren't going anywhere until someone returns all the stolen money."

He had the cash from his full house win inside his wallet, but he doubted the amount could even make a slight dent in what D.R. wanted. Dotty tucked her arm into his, folding into his side. As they were commanded to the car parked in the bushes, the revolver touched the back of his skull. "Where are you taking us?"

"Say goodbye to freedom."

"We can't miss breakfast!" Dotty cried out. Tears covered her flushed cheeks. He rubbed small circles on her back.

"It's a couple of hours north where we're headed." D.R. sunk back, whistling and tapping the steering wheel. A silvery moonbeam ricocheted off his chunky pinky ring.

He prayed for their freedom, and Dotty buried her face in his collar.

DOTTY

"Please go slower," she cried. If not for Abe beside her, she would have fainted by now. The cigar smoke was making her eyes burn.

D.R. hit the gas pedal with intent. Pebbles hit the side of the car as they sped forward.

She prayed throughout the entire drive inside the black Pontiac Streamliner. She had also been sending telepathic SOS messages to anyone who might be receptive. The car jerked to a stop in front of a large house with peeling white paint and a rickety banister.

"Get out," instructed D.R., his revolver back in his right hand while he picked something off the passenger seat cushion. "Mother is always losing these things," he tossed the large hairpin onto the dashboard.

She catapulted out of the car as a crucial piece of the puzzle fell into place. She froze and bent over with her hands on her knees, gulping mountain air into her lungs.

"Follow me," growled D.R.

Abe reached for her hand. Still frozen in fear, he nudged her up the seedy porch steps with a soft touch. "Is Hershel inside?" he asked.

"I already told you I don't know where he is. Until you figure out how to return all the money, you'll be my hostages." D.R. smacked his lips together.

She tried to control her shaking legs as she stepped into the dim foyer, landing on a squeaky piece of the floor. A portrait of a young girl in a lacy dress stared at her from the wall. Everything about the place was creepy.

"Hershel!" Abe yelled.

She dug her fingernails into his arm—he ought to stay quiet.

The revolver was rammed into Abe's left shoulder. "Don't try any dirty tricks."

Her entire body was shaking like a leaf, and it was a miracle she managed to climb the decaying staircase without tripping. She prayed these were not her last moments alive.

They were forced into a cubbyhole at the end of the hallway. D.R. slid a bookcase in front of the opening to barricade them from escaping. Only after hearing his footsteps clomping down the stairs did she release the breath she had been holding. Already *schvitzing*, she ran her eyes over the broken fan in the corner. It was missing a blade and resting on its side.

Abe went to the window and tried to raise it while she cowered in place. She was picking at the loose thread on her beyond-repairable gown. The hole now exposed flesh from her waist to her rib cage.

"I expected Sy to save us. He knows we are in real danger. Where is he?" Abe yanked at one of the nails holding the window shut. Moments later, he managed to jimmy the window open and let out a holler.

She leaned out over the sloped edge of the roof and cried, "We have to get to the ground."

Suddenly, they heard the bookcase moving. They snapped back to attention, slid the window closed, and positioned themselves in front of it. They hoped it was not obvious that it had been meddled with.

D.R. popped into the small, humid room with a ceiling so low that if he stood up straight, he would bump his head. "I want the rest of the money." He held the revolver steady.

She squeezed Abe's hand and remained silent, staring at the nail that had fallen to the floor.

"I planned it so it would be Eva going on this journey. Funny how things work out and it was you two I nabbed instead." D.R. jerked the gun at Abe and clucked his tongue on the roof of his mouth. "Same thing happened with you after the fire."

D.R. stepped so close to Abe that they could share one straw in a single soda pop. "You're used to being collateral damage. Well, this time it's more serious; the stakes are at their peak."

In fear of vomiting again, she was *schvitzing* so much that she had to let go of Abe's hand to fan her face.

"I still can't figure out how Hershel escaped in that Cadillac the night of the fire. How did the driver time it so perfectly when the fire was a true accident?" D.R. put a hand to his heart. "Honest to God. Mother only wanted to feed the silly little cat. She went looking for it, couldn't see a thing with her cataracts, lit a match, ended up dropping it, and the rest is history."

Dotty put both hands over her mouth. The nightclub was not destroyed by gangsters or by arson after all. It was just an accident caused by a little old lady. Ordinarily, she would never trust him to tell the truth, but there was evidence to confirm his story.

"Mother saved you and Eva that night I dropped you off at the farm. I had to leave you to be by her side at the hospital. That allowed Sy the opportunity to swoop in." D.R. snarled at Abe and took a step back. "Mother is still in the hospital recovering from smoke inhalation. Luckily, my sister is back from her vacation and can take over Mother's care."

Just then, the front door slammed open. The sound of feet climbing the stairs startled D.R. so much that he knocked his head on the ceiling. Arms extended, he held the gun with two hands and lunged out of the cubbyhole.

Abe rushed to open the window and then bumped Dotty onto the roof, ensuring she landed safely. With adrenaline pumping, she balanced herself on the sloped edge. She heard the engine of a car and stared down at it. "Let that be our escape car," she prayed with all her might.

A gunshot rang through the air. She prayed more. Abe slipped on a roof shingle. Another gunshot went off, and bile rose in her throat. She smelled the blood in the air and vomited off the side of the roof. D.R.'s whimpers drained the remaining color left in her cheeks.

Abe had his eyes focused on the embankment to the right. She followed his gaze and immediately squeezed her eyes shut. A wheelbarrow carrying the body of their kidnapper, splayed inside it, was rolling toward the creek. The sight of all that blood had her wanting to vomit more.

Abe held an arm out, preventing her from injury while blocking her body from whoever was sticking his hands out of the open window. She clung to his arm for dear life. "Sy!" she gasped. God answered her prayers.

"I was on your tail the entire time." He pulled her inside.

"What about Hershel? Is he being held here?" Abe asked, edging himself into the cubbyhole.

Sy was silent as he guided them out of the house. Dotty was afraid to loosen her death grip on Abe as she descended the unsteady staircase. She kept her eyes straight ahead so as not to see the wheelbarrow ever again. Abe pushed her from behind once more, this time into the escape car, and Sy sped them away.

A safe distance away, a figure popped out of the front seat and stuck his head into the back.

"Hershel!" Abe and Dotty yelled at an ear-splitting level.

She relaxed for the first time since the nightmare began.

"Where have you been, pal?" Abe asked.

Hershel and Sy exchanged glances.

"You see, I knew I needed to disappear for a couple of days because D.R. was turning up the heat on his money hunt. I feared I was about a day away from someone throwing me into a lake. Look what happened to the Rio Cabana; I didn't want someone to turn me into ashes next," Hershel said.

She wrinkled her nose at the image.

"Marv had been counting inventory later than usual that night. It was a random streak of luck that he was in the right place at the right time to save me. He felt bad he couldn't save you, too, Abey. Marv drove me straight to his cabin in Rochester."

Abe twisted his expression around. Dotty picked sequins off her gown. And Sy took over the storytelling. "I uncovered information that D.R. bought a house up here to be closer to Jack Drucker while he was in prison."

She remembered the morning Sy had eaten breakfast at her table. He had mentioned a drive upstate. She leaned back, stunned by all she was learning.

Sy glanced at her. "When you let me have the button you found near the Rio C, I traced it back to Marv and his navy vest."

She pictured Marv's vest with all those buttons. "Ah ha." She knew she recognized the button.

"Marv admitted he had played a role in Hershel's disappearance, and I promised to stay quiet. It wasn't until later in the week that Marv contacted me in a panic." Sy took his eyes off the road to glare at Hershel.

Hershel kept his eyes locked on the road ahead.

"The plan was for Marv to drive to Rochester on Tuesday to bring Hershel back to the Concord. But this time, Hershel really was missing in action." Sy glared once more.

Hershel flashed a goofy grin. "What can I say? The plan went haywire. I lost track of time. I always intended to make my way back for the big show."

Sy rolled his eyes. "I did some more investigating. I found that 'the Casanova of the Concord' met a waitress twice his age and shacked up with her. It probably wasn't the smartest idea messin' with the local pig farmer's wife."

"Please don't tell Eva," Hershel said. He made puppy dog eyes.

She turned her head toward the window, woozy from so much information to absorb.

Sy continued. "I tailed D.R.'s car the entire way here, took a quick pit stop to grab Hershel, and then we pulled off your rescue."

She asked a pertinent question: "What happened to the money?"

"I don't want a penny of that dirty *gelt* anymore. Let it ruin someone else's life." Hershel flared his nostrils.

She ran her eyes over Hershel's soiled clothing and saw traces of blood splattered on his trousers. She trembled against Abe's side.

"Sit back, kids, and take a rest. You've been through a lot." Sy turned on a jazz station.

"We already missed breakfast," she said, discouraged.

"We'll be lucky if we make dinner," said Abe.

"As long as I'm back in time to work Danny Kaye's show," said Hershel.

She did not have the heart to break it to him that he was no longer employed at the Concord. "I absolutely cannot miss Saturday dinner," is all she said.

Chapter 25

ABE

The traffic had stopped for an eternity, making Abe so anxious that he feared he might have a heart attack. For the first hour, after learning it had been a centenarian responsible for the fire, he sat in shock. Now he was worried about Leon manning the staff dining room alone. Hershel snoring in the front seat gave him one huge thing to be glad about—they had rescued him safe and sound.

Sy finally drove past the accident. Dotty's tears continued as she watched the gruesome scene. He said a prayer for the injured people.

Sy increased the speed. "Hold tight."

He leaned his head back, resolved to whatever fate awaited him. Dotty's tears turned into hiccups.

As the lights of the Concord came into view, he and Dotty both tensed. Sy breezed through the gates with a salute to the guard. Abe whisked Dotty out of the car, offering his jacket to cover the bare skin on her midriff. He hoped Moss Hart was not near to see the poor condition of the emerald-green gown.

Hershel barreled toward the dining room. It was transformed into the showroom for Danny Kaye's act. His appearance drew everyone's attention. Abe worried about everything as he followed him.

The soprano singer on stage held a low note for the crowd, which was mostly made up of standing people. Dotty's trembling hands held onto his arm as they saw Eva openly intertwined with Leon.

Hershel made a beeline straight for the pair. The singer bowed to thunderous applause as Hershel lunged at Leon. Abe hurried to break up the fight, bumping into a cocktail waitress. He steadied her tray of water glasses and then raced to the battle. Leon panted as Hershel had his hands around his neck, strangling him, yelling, "You're a *schmuck*!"

Irving took hold of Hershel's arm. He yanked him away as Eva whacked Hershel with her wrist bag.

"I was sick with worry!" yelled Leon, his breath jagged, throwing his arms around Abe.

His glasses got knocked to the floor. "I'm all right, pal. How are you holding up?" Abe snatched his glasses up before someone stepped on them.

Hershel sprang onto a tabletop and screamed, "I'm back at the Concord, baby!" He hurled himself down and scooped Eva into his arms.

Abe put his glasses back on in time to see Eva wiggling out of Hershel's embrace. Hershel then threw another punch at Leon's face.

Arthur rose from his front-row seat. Irving shoved Hershel out of the showroom as the lights went pitch black, and Danny Kaye rocketed onto the stage.

"Let's go," Dotty said, grabbing his hand before the first punchline.

They were near the exit when someone tapped him on the arm. He whipped around, fists balled, jaw clenched. "Mr. Berg, I don't have the autograph yet. I will get it over breakfast. I promise." He pasted a semi-smile on his face and hoped he wasn't telling a lie.

Mr. Berg slumped his shoulders.

In the hallway, he gasped at the same time as Dotty. A furious Hershel pinned Al Beckman, one-half of the dynamic talent bookers Winarick had hired, down on the floor. Eva was throwing a tantrum, and Leon was sitting on the sidelines with a split lip.

"You're all fired!" Irving yelled over the noise. "I don't want to see any of you in my dining room again."

DOTTY

Dotty had shed a bucket full of tears. Oh, how disappointed Ma and Papa would be with her for losing her job.

"Don't worry, Dot, there are many hotels in the area. Any of them would be lucky to hire you as a waitress." Shock lined Abe's face.

She was already so attached to the Concord. Her spirit sank. She sniffled and wiped away more tears. Abe was massaging her back. The sweet gesture caused her heart to skip a beat. He, too, had lost his livelihood, and his stakes were even higher. Her eyes followed Hershel chasing Al Beckman down the hallway. She was glad he had finished throwing punches at Leon.

"Irving fired the cream of the crop in the dining room. Is he going to start carrying stations all on his own?" Eva sparked up a Lucky Strike and tapped her foot in nervous repetition.

Leon was on high alert, standing next to Eva, pressing a raw piece of meat to the cut on his lip. "Maybe the Nevele will hire us."

Eva flicked the ashes of the Lucky Strike into the fern beside her. "I heard the Laurels in Sackett Lake and the new Brown's Hotel that opened in Loch Sheldrake need waitresses."

"This is all your fault," Dotty sneered at the person she considered her best friend since day one of arriving at the Concord.

"Hershel caused all the trouble." Eva took a long drag on her Lucky Strike.

She did not disagree. She needed her own cigarette. Anxious for the nicotine to take effect, it took her several tries before she could get the match to light.

The dance team strutted by, and the strawberry-blonde dancer paused, shooting daggers at Abe. He did not even notice because he was helping Leon.

Eva's comment about the off-season's short-lived romances and fistfights rang in her ears. It wasn't even the middle of summer, and those things were already happening. She took another drag. She would no longer have to worry about anything that happened after Labor Day. Even if she somehow convinced Papa to let her stay, it was no longer an option.

The tallest dancer halted in front of Eva and placed her hand on her hip. Her New Jersey accent was strong; she asked, "Which mountain rat will you choose?"

The question was a good one, and the tension was as thick as the cottage cheese served at breakfast. Dotty was on pins and needles, waiting for the answer. Eva looked at the dancer, then turned and walked the other way.

Sy was shuffling over to speak with Abe. "The first meeting is Wednesday," he said.

Unable to hear Abe's response because of the audience's laughter, she wished to be blissfully watching the show instead of feeling humiliated for losing her job.

Sy slapped Abe on the back and slunk away. She

poked her finger into Abe's shoulder. "How come you are always mixed up in no-good stuff?"

"What are you talking about, Dot?"

"Sy is a criminal."

"He just saved our lives."

"He just killed someone."

"I think he deserves a lot of credit for rescuing us and driving us back here." Abe reached for her hand. "Let's sneak back into the show. We can still catch a joke or two."

She shook her head, incapable of finding humor in a set of jokes right now. Fearful about her future and craving comfort, she let him hold her hand. He then steered them out of the nearest exit. Boychik, wearing a new green collar, greeted them with a single meow as if to say welcome back. The moon was a sliver, surrounded by sparkling stars. She breathed in the rich floral scent coming from the garden and tried to calm the jitters in her stomach. Abe put his hand under her chin, tilting her face upward. A warmth spread through her body as she gazed into his chocolatey eyes. She melted into his body, passionately returning his kiss.

A rush of joy replaced her despair until Sy hollered out. "Abey, I forgot to tell you we'll be meeting inside the Wunderbar in Fallsburg."

She stepped backward. Unsure if she wanted to pursue a relationship where dancers and gangsters caused her such unease, she touched her fingers to her lips. They were still tingling from her first kiss in the mountains. She figured it would also be her last kiss there.

CHAPTER 26
1 Week Later

ABE AND DOTTY

Hershel held his spiral-bound notebook. He was charging through the lobby. "Judy Garland is booked here in two weeks!" he yelled.

Dotty swooned. Abe furrowed his brows. His ma would dash back to the mountains when she learned that one of her favorite actresses was performing at the Concord.

Strolling hand in hand to the Colonial, they saw Leon carrying a can of tuna. He entered the staff quarters ahead of them.

"How long is Boychik going to live in your room?" Dotty asked.

Abe did not mind the tiny cat bunking with them until the new nightclub was built, but it made Dotty sneeze, so she could not visit their room. He hoped to spend lots of time with her all year long now that she had been hired to waitress for every season.

To their left, Eva jogged by, a new deck of cards in hand. "You don't have much time before we have to be at dinner," Dotty hollered to her friend, who did not slow her pace one bit.

Thankfully, Irving had needed their help so desperately that he had rescinded their terminations by lunchtime the next day.

They heard a car tooting its horn and saw Sy waving goodbye. "I'm off to Atlantic City. Try to stay out of trouble while I'm away, kids."

Dotty waved a jubilant goodbye and nuzzled into

Abe's neck. She had been ecstatic when her papa had allowed her to withdraw from City College. She created a life in the mountains, and she intended to stay here forever.

Inside the sundry shop, where they stopped for a couple of postcards, Marv gave them a knowing smile. He threw two Tootsie Pops into the bag. "On the house for your part in the recent state of affairs." He wore his navy vest with all six buttons back in place.

"Let's go get an egg cream," Abe said.

Dotty fluttered her eyelashes and grabbed his hand. An exciting future lay ahead in the mountains.

EPILOGUE

It was another moonless night; the deepest part of the creek submerged the wheelbarrow. Someone stuffed D.R.'s lifeless body inside the trunk of the car, and the metal safe rested on the passenger seat. With enough gas to reach Monticello, the sedan chugged there. Snores came from the back seat.

Acknowledgments

This book has been in the works for a long time. I tried to make it as historically accurate as I could. I've had the pleasure of speaking with Borscht Belt hotel owners, employees, guests, children of the workers who ran through the hallways at all hours of the day, and many others along the way.

My first thank you is to my late great-aunt, Jean Barrish, the original writer in the family. Without her written memories about the tumultuous childhood with my great-grandmother and living in foster care, there would be no recollection. I'm picturing my aunt right now with her joyful smile cheering me on.

Kandace Ayala, I don't think I could have done this without you. Your dedication to helping me reach this dream is like no other. You always listened and offered research-based advice. It was truly a gift to me. Thank you for loving my grandparents. If only we still had Dot's dresses that we used to wear when we played dress-up as children.

Cassandra Bell, thank you for beta reading and for your encouragement. Together we drove through Philadelphia and located Grandpa Abe's childhood home. We sure had some fun times with my grandparents at their home in Delray Beach—and ate lots of matzo ball soup. You will forever be known as "Samantha" to Dot.

Meredith Schorr, thank you for being in my corner and sharing your writing journey with me.

John Conway, thank you for your support and for leading by example.

Patti Posner, thank you for helping me get the dining room and food information correct. I'm fortunate to be able to lean on a former hotelier and fellow author.

Erica Shawn Gold and Barry Gold, thank you for your enthusiasm and for stepping in to edit when I needed you.

Richard and Jackie Chiger, thank you for sharing your Yiddish expertise with me.

Myron Gittell, I called you with many, many questions, and you had the answers. Thank you.

Mom and Dad, I could never have made my dreams come true without your support every step of the way. THANK YOU! And thank you for preserving Grandma and Grandpa's hotel memorabilia.

Grandma Dotty and Grandpa Abe, I know you two are dancing in the clouds over my debut. Thank you for being the best grandparents to me. Some of my favorite memories are of spending time with you in the Catskills.

Grandma Maryanne and Grandpa Bill, thank you for also being the best grandparents to me and believing in me as a writer since day one.

Maggie, Matt, Cameron, June, and Isaac, our special family history is now shared with the world. Thank you for being a part of it.

Nick Mullan, you are a star proofreader—thank you for all your help as a colleague and friend.

Rachel Carrigan and Kadeidra Deas, thank you for setting aside time to meet with me. I need our tech team coffee club.

Karen Miller, I can't thank you enough for everything you did for my book. I'm so lucky I met you at the writing retreat in Princeton.

Lucia Macro, thank you for offering advice and giving me confidence. It was kismet meeting in grad school.

Wendy Corsi Staub, thank you for blurbing my book even when you were as busy as a bee. You are an inspiration.

Camille Di Maio, thank you for your thoughtful beta reader suggestions. It was your idea to create a certain storyline, and my book is better because of it.

Jaycee DeLorenzo and Lisa Snyder, thank you for your patience with my website and graphics as I figure all of this out.

Thank you to my early readers: Marilyn Simon Rothstein, Thelma Adams, Eva Hnizdo, and Sheila Myers.

Thank you to Ira Simon, the Whites, and everyone else who helped in some capacity. I appreciate you all.

A huge thank you to all my book friends and readers.

I read so many Facebook comments on all the wonderful sites devoted to the Borscht Belt era. Thank you to all who posted their memories on social media for me to read. The ones that mentioned my grandparents warmed my heart.

My *bashert*, Jeremy Levner, who it turns out is a fantastic editor! We share a similar history. Both of our grandparents worked at the Concord. Your eagle eye for even the smallest details has made my novel more authentic. You make my life better every single day. Thank you.

About the Author

Lily Barrish Levner comes from a family that cherished books and learning—her mother was a schoolteacher, and her father was the director of the Monticello library, so it's no surprise that storytelling has always been a part of her life. Growing up in Kiamesha Lake, New York, Lily spent her childhood sleuthing around the iconic Catskills resorts with friends and soaking up the vibrant atmosphere. Her grandparents worked in the resort industry, a connection that inspires her stories.

As a fourth-generation Jewish American, Lily deeply connects to the Catskill Mountains and the Borscht Belt, where her heritage and childhood memories blend. Her fondest recollections are tied to places like the Concord, Kutsher's, the Pines, the Raleigh, and Sunny Oaks bungalow colony—sites that have left an indelible mark on her writing.

With a BA in Creative Writing and a Master's in Library and Information Science, Lily has spent the past decade as a copy desk researcher at *Bloomberg Businessweek* while working on her novel and contributing monthly articles to the *Hurleyville Sentinel*. She currently lives in the Catskills with her husband and their dog, Gus, where the magic of the mountains still influences her work.

Stay tuned for the further adventures of Dotty and Abe when Book 2 of the *Catskills Capers* series is published in the summer of 2025.